ACCLAIM FOR *Peter Ackroyd*'s

The Plato Papers

"Peter Ackroyd is a visionary, as *The Plato Papers* makes clear. This is one of the oddest but most important novels to appear in many years. This masterpiece of contemporary writing will thrill and entertain readers for years to come, but it will do more than that: it will enlarge their vision, stimulating organs long forgotten and never known."

> —Jay Parini, author of *The Last Station* and *Robert Frost: A Life*

"[*The Plato Papers*] makes an easy introduction to an author who, like Plato, questions the century's most treasured assumptions. Insidiously, he persuades readers to doubt them, too."
> —*San Francisco Chronicle*

"A work that manages to be at once metaphysical romp, vaudeville routine, survey of human history, and satire on contemporary society and smug academics."
> —*The Seattle Times*

"What makes [*The Plato Papers*] notable is not its fantastic invention but its intelligence. . . . Excellently written . . . with a truly Socratic curiosity, making *The Plato Papers* a philosophical good read."
> —Malcolm Bradbury, *Financial Times*

"Ackroyd is such a wonderful writer, his sentences pop with wit and weight. This newest book is intellectual *and* entertaining, no small accomplishment."
> —*The Commercial Appeal* (Memphis)

Peter Ackroyd

The Plato Papers

Peter Ackroyd is the award-winning author of the national bestseller *The Life of Thomas More*. His biographies—including *T. S. Eliot*, *Dickens*, and *Blake*—are as prized as his novels, which include *Chatterton*, *Hawksmoor*, and, most recently, *The Trial of Elizabeth Cree* and *Milton in America*. He lives in London.

ALSO BY PETER ACKROYD

FICTION

The Great Fire of London
The Last Testament of Oscar Wilde
Hawksmoor
Chatterton
First Light
English Music
The House of Doctor Dee
The Trial of Elizabeth Cree
Milton in America

BIOGRAPHY

T. S. Eliot
Dickens
Blake
The Life of Thomas More

POETRY

The Diversions of Purley

CRITICISM

Notes for a New Culture

THE

Plato☉

Papers

a prophesy

ANCHOR BOOKS

A Division of Random House, Inc.

New York

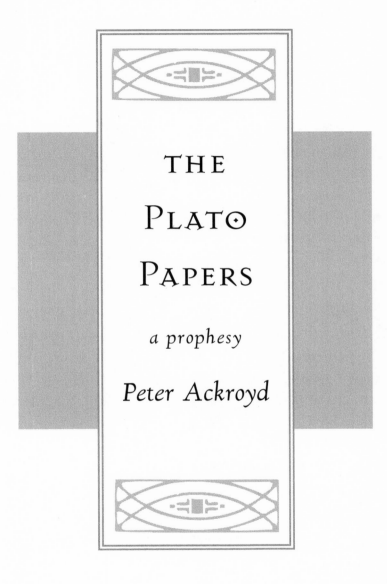

THE

PLATO

PAPERS

a prophesy

Peter Ackroyd

FIRST ANCHOR BOOKS EDITION, MARCH 2001

The Library of Congress has cataloged the Nan A. Talese
edition as follows:
Ackroyd, Peter, 1949–
The Plato papers: a prophesy / Peter Ackroyd.
—1st ed. in the U.S.A.
p.   cm.
ISBN 0-385-49768-7
I. Title.
PR6051.C64P58   2000
823'.914—dc21   99-16573
CIP

Anchor ISBN: 0-385-49769-5

Author photograph © Roderick Field
Book design by Dana Leigh Treglia

www.anchorbooks.com

Printed in the United States of America
10   9   8   7   6   5   4   3   2   1

For Elizabeth Wyndham

c. 3500 BC–c. 300 BC: The Age of Orpheus
c. 300 BC–c. AD 1500: The Age of the Apostles
c. AD 1500–c. AD 2300: The Age of Mouldwarp
c. AD 2300–c. AD 3400: The Age of Witspell
c. AD 3700: The Present

I often envisage, in this new age of universal and instantaneous communication, how our planet might appear to distant observers. It must seem to shimmer in a state of continual excited activity, rather like a round diamond in the sky.

Ronald Corvo, A *New Theory of the Earth*, 2030.

All fallen dark and quiet, all gone down. Collapsophe.

Joseph P., *Diaries*, 2299.

We who survive, we scoured ones, in depths of dark dismay, call out of the night of our world, gone as we knew it, as we know it.

London hymn, c. 2302.

Slivers of light. Silvers. Little horn-shaped lights, riding the waves of darkness.

Joseph P., *Diaries*, 2304.

Myander, a Londoner, wrote the history of a changing world, beginning at the moment of transition, believing that it would mark a great epoch, one more worthy of relation than any that had come before. This belief was not without its grounds. The world of science had collapsed, but the divine consciousness of humanity had not yet asserted itself. All the labours of Myander lay in recording the manifest signs of dismay and wonder. Since the events of distant antiquity, even those immediately preceding the great change, cannot clearly be understood she believed it her duty to enquire carefully into immediate circumstances.

Myander, *History*, 2310.

The holy city, restored. Ourselves, revived.

Proclamation, 2350.

The components of the light have been carefully studied. In addition to manifold influences on the human plane, such as will and desire, there are tokens of power from the earth itself. The smallest territory can exert its influence, moving those who come within its boundaries. This city, for example, is not indifferent to the joys or sufferings of its inhabitants.

The London Intelligencer, 2998.

I cannot pretend to have been present during the glorious restoration of human light, the greatest and perhaps most significant scene in the narrative of humankind. Yet I believe that I am blessed in another sense, living on the verge of a new age. All around me I am beginning to see greatness and munificence erected, while our citizens with wonderful zeal have tried to revive and emulate the labours of distant antiquity. When asked why they are engaged in this pursuit, they reply 'Why not? What else is there to do?' This is our new spirit!

Letter from Popcorn to Mellitus, 3399.

The city bears us. The city loves its burden. Nurture it in return. Do not leave its bounds.

Proclamation, 3506.

In returning to the origin of all things, we meet our destiny. Do you see our doubles, passing by us weeping? This is the nature of our world.

Proverbs of Restituta, guardian of London, 3640.

It is sometimes considered wayward or importunate to paint a portrait of one man, yet we know from the pictures of parishioners lit upon the Wall of our great and glorious city that a single feature or glance may embody a fateful moment or an eventful transaction. So I intend to conjure up a likeness of Plato, the great orator of London, in a similar fashion. I will practise the art of selection; like the displays of our actors continually before us, some events will be presented on a grand scale and others diminished. The conventions of spherical drama will be preserved from the beginning to the end; the revelations and lamentations, for example, will be in strict keeping with each other. By these means we may see his unhappily brief life as a continual search after truth. But it will also be my duty faithfully to record Plato's final days in the city and to ascertain how a cruel superstition excercised boundless dominion over the most elevated and benevolent mind.

Anon., The Plato Papers, 3705.

THE

Plato

Papers

a prophesy

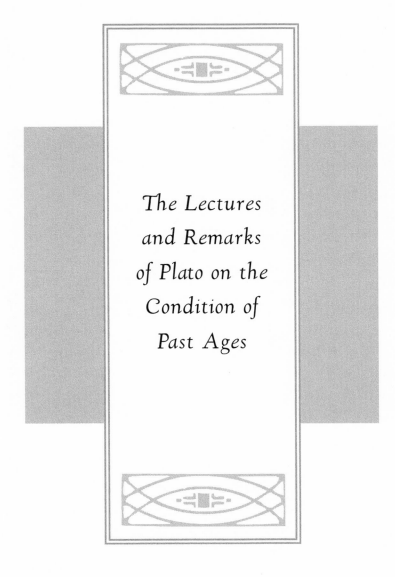

*The Lectures
and Remarks
of Plato on the
Condition of
Past Ages*

I

Sparkler: Wait, Sidonia, wait!

Sidonia: Gladly.

Sparkler: I just saw you in the market. You were standing beneath the city wall, and so I assumed that you were listening to Plato's oration.

Sidonia: Correct in every respect, Sparkler. But I expected to see you there, since you always celebrate the feast of Gog.

Sparkler: I was about to cross the Fleet, and join you, when Madrigal stopped me.

Sidonia: What did he want?

Sparkler: Only something about a parish meeting. But, as a result, I missed Plato's opening remarks. I heard only his ending, when he spoke of his sorrow at the darkness of past ages.

Sidonia: It was all very interesting. There was a period when our ancestors believed that they inhabited a world which revolved around a sun.

Sparkler: Can it be true?

Sidonia: Oh yes. They had been told that they lived upon a spherical planet, moving through some kind of infinite space.

Sparkler: No!

Sidonia: That was their delusion. But it was the Age of Mouldwarp. According to Plato, the whole earth seemed to have been reduced and rolled into a ball until it was small enough to fit their theories.

Sparkler: But surely they must have known—or felt?

Sidonia: They could not have known. For them the sun was a very powerful god. Of course we were all silent for a moment, after Plato had told us this, and then he laughed.

Sparkler: He laughed?

Sidonia: Even when he had taken off the orator's mask, he was still smiling. Then he began to question us. 'Do you consider me to be small? I know that you do. Could you imagine the people of Mouldwarp to be much, much smaller? Their heads were tiny, and their

4

eyes like pinpoints. Do you know,' he said, 'that in the end they believed themselves to be covered by a great net or web?'

Sparkler: Impossible. I never know when Plato is telling the truth.

Sidonia: That is what he enjoys. The game. That is why he is an orator.

Sparkler: We who have known him since child-hood—

Sidonia: —never cease to wonder.

Sparkler: But who could be convinced by such wild speculations?

Sidonia: Come and decide for yourself. Walk with me to the white chapel, where he is about to begin his second oration.

2

I will speak of a novelist, Charles Dickens, who flour-
ished in a period somewhere between the seventeenth
and twentieth centuries of our earth. The titles of
his works have been retrieved but only one text sur-
vives, alas in an incomplete form. Seven pages have
been removed, and the author's name partially defaced, for reasons which are unknown to me. Most
of the narrative remains, however, and it provides a
unique opportunity to examine the nature of Mouldwarp imagination. The novel is entitled *On the Origin*

of Species by Means of Natural Selection, by Charles D——.
The rest of the name has been gouged out by some
crude tool, and the phrase 'Vile stuff!' written in a
dye-based substance. Clearly the reader did not ap-
prove of the fiction! Perhaps it was too melodramatic,
or romantic, for her refined taste! Despite this erasure,
we have no cause to doubt that this novel was composed by the author of *Great Expectations* and *Hard
Times*.

It opens with a statement by the hero of the
narrative—'When on board HMS *Beagle*, as a naturalist, I was much struck with certain facts . . .'—
who then proceeds to tell his remarkable story. By
observing bees, and pigeons, and various other creatures around him, he manages to create within his own
mind an entire world of such complexity that eventually he believes it to be real. This is reminiscent of another fiction we have recovered, *Don Quixote,* in which
the protagonist is similarly deluded. The quixotic hero
of *The Origin*, however, is portrayed as being obsessed
by 'struggle', 'competition', and 'death by natural selection', in a manner both morbid and ludicrous. He
pretends to be exact in his calculations but then de-
clares that 'I have collected a long list of such cases but
here, as before, I lie under a great disadvantage in not
being able to give them'. This wonderfully comic re-
mark is succeeded by one no less rich in inadvertent
humour. 'It is hopeless', he states, 'to attempt to convince anyone of the truth of this proposition without

giving the long array of facts I have collected, and which cannot possibly be here introduced.' Here is a character who, if real, would not have been believed!

The subtlety of Charles Dickens's fiction now becomes apparent. In the act of inventing this absurd fellow, this 'naturalist' travelling upon the extraordinarily named *Beagle*, he has managed indirectly to parody his own society. The subtitle of the novel itself suggests one of the objects of his satire—'The Preservation of Favoured Races in the Struggle for Life' refers to the Mouldwarp delusion that all human beings could be classified in terms of 'race', 'gender' or 'class'. We find interesting evidence of this in the anecdotes of a comedian, Brother Marx, of whom I will speak at a later date. Yet Dickens is able to mock this eccentric hypothesis through the words of his hapless narrator, who suggests that 'widely ranging species which have already triumphed over many competitors . . . will have the best chance of seizing on new places when they spread into new countries'. It should be recalled that in the middle period of Mouldwarp the separate nations fought and colonised each other; as our hero puts it in his usual bland fashion, 'the northern forms were enabled to beat the less powerful southern forms' with the purpose 'of being victorious in distant lands in the struggle for life with foreign associates'. It is the final masterstroke of irony by Charles Dickens that his character solemnly maintains the pretence of discussing only birds and insects, while at the same time providing a wonderfully succinct if brutal summary of the society from which he came!

His is a dark world indeed, dominated by the necessity of labour and the appetite for power. Even the bees are 'anxious . . . to save time', and the protagonist extols 'the more efficient workshops of the north'; nature itself is described as frugal or even miserly, with a continual desire 'to economise'! Yet, in a transitional chapter of this novel, the hero ceases to be merely comic and reveals more malign or sinister characteristics. He suggests the need for 'heavy destruction' and announces, with no irony at all, 'let the strongest live and the weakest die'. In one remarkable passage he celebrates the spectacle of violent death—'we ought to admire', he informs us, 'the savage instinctive hatred of the queen bee, which instantly urges her to destroy the young queens, her daughters'. We have come across fragments of writing—'the death of queens', 'queens have died young and fair'—which suggest that he is here alluding to a dramatic tradition now lost to us. But nothing can disguise his own interest in carnage.

Combat and slaughter, in fact, become the principal components of the unreal world which he has created. He imagines all life on earth to be derived from one 'common parent' or 'primordial form'; the offspring of this 'prototype' then develop into various species of animal or plant, which in turn fight among themselves in order to 'progress towards perfection'. He calls it 'evolution'. No laughter, please. He is only the protagonist of a novel! Well, laugh if you must. But remember that Charles Dickens himself is satirising the blind pretensions of his era. Remember, too, that no one from this dark past could have known that all aspects of the world change suddenly and that new organic life appears when the earth demands it. Only in the Age of Witspell, for example, was it realised that the petrified shapes found in rock or ice were created to mock or mimic their organic counterparts. In the same period it was also recognised that each portion of the earth produces its own creatures spontaneously.

I will conclude this oration with a theme introduced by the novel itself. Even as the protagonist concludes his false and rambling description of the natural world, he reflects upon his own experience in lugubrious terms. 'How fleeting are the wishes and efforts of man,' he complains, 'how short his time!' These are typical Mouldwarp sentiments but, on this occasion, they come from a deluded scholar who claimed to understand the motive power behind such general 'wishes and efforts'! May I recommend *The Origin of Species* to you, then, as a comic masterpiece?

3

Madrigal: Did you enjoy the oration?

Ornatus: Immensely. Even the angels seemed interested, especially when Plato mentioned that theory—that thing—what was it?

Madrigal: Convolution?

Ornatus: Precisely. Convolutions. I had to laugh.

Madrigal: We all did. But why are the beliefs of our ancestors so ridiculous? I am sure that they were sincerely held.

Ornatus: No doubt.

Madrigal: Perhaps, in the future, someone might laugh at—well—you and me.

Ornatus: There is nothing funny about us.

Madrigal: As far as we know.

Ornatus: A good point. We must ask Plato about this as soon as possible. To think that in our schooldays we were all in the same parish—you, me, Plato.

Madrigal: And Sparkler. How could you forget Sparkler? With his long robe and white hair.

Ornatus: And Sidonia, too, with her red hair and the blue light shining from her.

Madrigal: I have known them so long that sometimes they seem very close, and sometimes in the far distance.

Ornatus: All human perception is a dream. Or so Plato tells us. And there he is by the clerk's well. He seems to be talking to himself.

Madrigal: Impossible. He must be practising his next oration.

4

Plato: How do I know that you are my soul?

Soul: How do you know that I am not?

Plato: I have been taught that our souls exist, of course, but this is the first time you have decided to appear.

Soul: It is unusual, I admit, but not wholly unprecedented. I can prove that I am your soul, by the way. Look at this.

Plato: Is it truly? Oh, my mother. Can I touch——?

Soul: No. It is not allowed. Now look what you have done. She has faded.

Plato: How is it possible? How did you summon her?

Soul: Her own soul was a close companion of mine. We used to talk and sing, when you and your mother were sitting together.

Plato: She was always wreathed in white.

Soul: That was the colour of the city in those days.

Plato: We had an old house, built of light and not of stone.

Soul: I remember it well. That was where it all began, I suppose.

Plato: Began?

Soul: Do you always ask questions? It may become irritating. She used to tell you stories. Fables and legends of the old time.

Plato: So I became aware of the city and its history.

Soul: So you did.

Plato: And so I studied.

Soul: So-so. You were chosen as orator, at least.

Plato: No other citizen desired the office. It is not considered quite proper to dwell upon the past, as I do. It is not appropriate. Yet they attend the orations, and listen politely.

Soul: Or laugh.

Plato: I enjoy their laughter. I am their clown. I protect them from doubt about themselves. Even when I speak the truth, I am so small that they do not consider my words of much importance.

Soul: You always speak the truth, as far as you understand it.

Plato: And, presumably, that is not very far.

Soul: I am not permitted to dwell upon such things. You are becoming. I am being. There is a difference. I wish that I could help you with your glossary of ancient terms, for instance, but it is forbidden. I cannot intervene.

Plato: How did you know about——?

Soul: You must have realised by now that we have a very intimate relationship. Well, if you will excuse me, I think I ought to rest for a while. May I just slip away quietly?

Plato: Do you think anyone has noticed you?

Soul: Of course not. You have been staring into space, and talking to yourself. That is all.

5

antibiotic: a death ray of the Mouldwarp era.

biographer: from bio-graphy, the reading of a life by means of lines. A fortune-teller or palmist.

brainstorm: on certain occasions the amount of anger or anxiety in the brain was believed to cause a violent change in the weather.

CD: an abbreviation of 'cold dirge', a form of music designed to calm or deaden human faculties.

common sense: a theory that all human beings might

be able to share one another's thoughts, so that there would in reality be only one person upon the earth.

cost of living: a phrase used to denote signs of weariness or debility; thus 'Can you calculate her cost of living?'

daylight saving: a technique by which light was stored in great containers and then taken through underground pipes to the residences of Mouldwarp.

dead end: a place where corpses were taken. One such site has been located at Shadow-well or Shade-well in the east of the old city. Another has been found at Mortlake. Those who chose to inhabit these areas apparently suffered from a 'death wish'.

decadence: a belief in the recurrence of the decades so that, for example, the 2090s resembled the 1990s, which in turn recalled the 1890s. It is a theory that has never been wholly disproved and it retained certain adherents even in the Age of Witspell.

echology: the practice of listening to the sound of one's own voice, as if it then became of greater importance.

economics: an ancient science, devoted to reducing all phenomena to their smallest and most niggardly point. Hence 'to practise economy' was synonymous with 'miserliness'.

electricity: a doubtful term but one generally thought to represent the element of fire or heat, as distinguished from moisture and cold. It was, therefore, a debased version of astral magic. In the earlier Age of Orpheus it was supposed that celestial bodies emanated a 'spiritual and divine light' which took 'a gracious passage through all things' with 'a reception by each, according to each one's capacity'. The nature of electricity suggests that this belief was somehow inherited by the people of Mouldwarp in a less holy and reverent form.

fibre optic: a coarse material woven out of eyes, worn by the high priests of the mechanical age in order to instil terror among the populace.

firewater: an unknown compound, perhaps related to the primitive superstition that there was a fire at the centre of all things. See 'electricity'.

flying saucers: a game for children. See also 'fast food'.

free will: a term of some significance in the Age of Mouldwarp, connected with the belief that individual choice or 'will' was of no value in a commercial market; it was therefore supplied free of charge.

globe: for many centuries the earth was perceived as a flattened disc at the centre of the universe; at a later date it was considered to be a spherical or rounded object circulating through space. A globe was a model designed to represent this last concept, although its proportions were evidently taken from the laws of geometrical harmony. Thus it resembled the magical orbus of the astrologer.

GMT: a hieroglyph discovered on several artefacts. It is believed to encode the ritualised worship of the god of mathematics and technology. See below.

god: in the Age of the Apostles, considered to be the supreme ruler of the universe. In the Age of Mould-warp, a mechanical and scientific genius. In the Age of Witspell, the principle of life reaching beyond its own limits.

half time: the circumstance or condition in which events seem to unfold very slowly, believed to represent a concerted effort of the Mouldwarp world to stop before it was too late.

ideology: the process of making ideas. The work was generally performed in silence and solitude, since great care was needed in their manufacture. Certain artisans were chosen for this occupation at an early age and were trained in mental workhouses or asylums. They were known as idealists, and were expected to provide a fixed number of ideas to be exhibited or dramatised for the benefit of the public.

ill wind: a wind that was sick, having been created by human perception.

information:

6

Sidonia: I believe that you were about to describe 'information'. May I sit with you, Plato, and discuss the subject?

Plato: By all means. Here in the cool and even light I feel sure that we will reach interesting conclusions. We sat here when we were children, debating the existence of light and the eternity of triangles.

Sidonia: You knew all the answers.

Plato: No. I knew the questions. I always wanted to catch your attention.

Sidonia: That was long ago.

Plato: Or a long way forward. Have you noticed how before and after have become strangely mingled? But this is idle chatter. You were asking me, were you not, about 'information'? By all accounts it was a very ancient deity. It conferred power upon those who worshipped it and was thought to have an invisible presence everywhere.

Sidonia: But what was the purpose of this god or spirit?

Plato: Apparently it had none. Even its devotees did not believe that they could become wiser, or happier, through its ministrations. In many respects it resembled the cults of Witspell which were performed only for the sake of the ceremonies themselves. Information simply granted its practitioners words and images.

Sidonia: Of what?

Plato: In that period it was believed that people should know of events far away, whether real or imagined.

Sidonia: Presumably this afforded them great benefits.

Plato: On the contrary. None at all. In fact it led to anxiety and bewilderment. But they persisted in the belief that it was necessary for them to suffer in these ways. They had been taught that they were the 'consumers' of the world.

Sidonia: But surely a consumer is one who eats?

Plato: Who devours. Consumers, as we know, are those who see this earth merely in relation to themselves; it only exists in the act of being ingested or enjoyed. Of course we have one or two consumers in the city, and they are kept apart from us, but can you imagine a whole society composed of these ravening creatures who thought of nothing but self-gratification?

Sidonia: A consumer society? It is impossible to imagine.

Plato: Yet they were never content, never fulfilled. Even as they were engaged in their ceaseless activity, they knew that it was futile.

Sidonia: But what was the nature of the events related to them?

Plato: It will be hard for you to accept what I am about to say.

Sidonia: In talking of ancient days, Plato, I have already learned to believe the impossible.

Plato: It appears likely, from all the available evidence, that the people of Mouldwarp loved chaos and disaster.

Sidonia: No!

Plato: It seems that they wished to learn of wars and murders; every kind of violation or despoilation delighted them. Information taught them to dissemble their pleasure, however, and in its service to retain an enquiring or sober countenance. Nevertheless they dwelled lovingly upon death and suffering. We believe that there were also 'papers' which chronicled all the worst incidents of the period and were distributed without charge to the populace.

Sidonia: Did everybody read this thing called papers?

Plato: It is hard to be sure. Of course no one derived any knowledge or wisdom from the activity. Difficult as it is for us to understand, they simply seemed to amuse themselves by reading about the misfortunes of others. This was the essential principle of information.

Sidonia: Would you suppose, then, that its worship was one of the reasons for the demise of the Age of Mouldwarp?

Plato: There can be little doubt of that. The dimming of the stars and the burning of instruments had many complex causes, but there is every reason to believe that the sacred cult of information was at least one of the symptoms of decline. Dark ceremonies and slavish pieties are characteristic of a decaying or diseased civilisation, and this religion of death may have rehearsed a more general dissolution. Now, if you will excuse me, Sidonia, I must return to my glossary.

7

iron age: the age of the machine. Known colloquially as the 'dark age', which in the end it became.

language laboratory: a sterile area where language was created under strict experimental conditions. New complex words or phrases were bred from existing phonetic and semantic systems before being tested upon a group of volunteers. There was of course always a danger of contamination or leakage; we believe that there were occasions when rogue words were accidentally released into the community, sometimes causing hysteria or fever.

literature: a word of unknown provenance, generally attributed to 'litter' or waste.

logic: a wooden object, as in log table.

nervous system: the system of Mouldwarp, in a state of continual anxiety. See 'nervous breakdown' for its eventual collapse.

old flame: it was once believed that the kindling of seasoned wood or the burning of an ancient house would inevitably produce old flames. But later research has suggested that the locality, rather than the material, is responsible for this phenomenon. That is why the citizens of Witspell noticed that fires started in familiar places; there were certain streets around the hall of the guilds, for example, where old flames periodically burst forth.

opening night: a reference to the creation myth of Mouldwarp, in which the universe is believed to have emerged from darkness and chaos; it was of course a theory that reflected the shadowy violence of the civilisation itself. The alternative, propounded by those few poets and prophets who rejected the culture of their period, seems to have been known as 'open day'. The phrase has been recognised in two or three fragments concerned with the education of the young.

organ grinder: a kind of butcher. See 'organism'.

pastoral: the reverence for the past, expressed by word of mouth.

pedestrian: one who journeyed on foot. Used as a term of abuse, as in 'this is a very pedestrian plot'. It is possible, therefore, that in ancient days walking was considered to be an ignoble or unnatural activity; this would explain the endless varieties of transport used to convey people for very short distances.

psychotic: a person in communion with his psyche or spirit, who sometimes spoke as if by inspiration.

question master: a grand official, or even leader. His role as interrogation master is not entirely clear, but it seems likely that he issued one or two questions a year to the general populace. The citizens would be expected to publish their answers, but he himself offered none.

recreation ground: an area of the city selected for the restoration of past life. See 'recognition' for the skills of those who performed this difficult procedure.

8

Sidonia: This is perhaps what Plato means by a recreation ground. Are you comfortable here? Let me raise an umbrella to protect you from the glare.

Ornatus: The sea is very troubled. I had not expected so many glimmers and flashes of light.

Sidonia: They are moments reappearing, little gleams of time in the general sea as countless as the grains of sand upon the beach. Shield your eyes and look over there. What is that emerging in the distance?

Ornatus: It must be some cloud of light, with its

form changing. It seems to take the shape of a face. No. It has become too wide. It is a magnificent building. Now it is breaking up into words.

Sidonia: It will change continually until it is drawn back into the sea. We believe that these configurations represent some great epoch, or century, struggling to regain existence. Sheaths of brightness have been observed, rising up from the sea with great rapidity before subsiding once more beneath the waves. These are the tokens of events, perhaps many thousands of years old, which have returned for an instant to the world's memory. There was the occasion when one great light left the people of this region dazed and bewildered. Some were reported to have spoken in strange languages and to have laughed or cried for no reason. Neighbours no longer recognised one another and members of the same family seemed strangers. But the anxiety passed. It was part of the process.

Ornatus: Surely the people of Mouldwarp also knew of this place? They gave it such a remarkable name.

Sidonia: Gravesend. But, according to Plato, it lay beneath their field of vision. This sea did not appear until Witspell, when the sun went out and the stars were dimmed. So many wonderful regions of the earth emerged in that period. There was one called Eden— Oh, look, your umbrella is falling down. Let me help you with it. Do you remember when we took part in the parish games? I helped you to find the light.

Ornatus: When we were small?

Sidonia: We had to go through the maze of glass—

Ornatus: And even though we could see perfectly, we were still lost!

Sidonia: Plato always held back, I think. Did he not run away before the dance?

Ornatus: He was afraid that he would break the glass.

Sidonia: But it cannot be broken. It is made from the tears of angels.

Ornatus: And as bright as the sea itself. Tell me, Sidonia. Has anyone entered this sea?

Sidonia: Let me put it this way: no one has ever returned.

Ornatus: But surely there was curiosity, as well as wonder? What if I were to throw my birth-plate into the water?

Sidonia: You are being facetious, I know, but it would also be very unwise. Let me tell you of one case. There was a young man from the village of Romford, not so far from here, who believed that the sea was an illusion and decided to test its powers. He walked down to the shore and looked at his reflection in the water.

Ornatus: Many of us do that. It is a question of achieving harmony for just one moment. I have seen Madrigal, for example, looking into the Lea with wonderful concentration.

Sidonia: Perhaps the reflection is our second self, as some people believe, but this is not the Lea. This is the sea of time. The villager stepped back and stood upon the sands, daring the waves to engulf him. When they refused the challenge, he ran towards them.

Ornatus: What happened?

Sidonia: He was seen to walk a short distance on the water and then to make great bounds, leaping high into the air.

Ornatus: How extraordinary!

Sidonia: On the first bound he turned into an ox, on the second into a swan; then he became in turn a snake, a lion and many other creatures, until he vanished from sight altogether.

Ornatus: All this is true?

Sidonia: All is true. Perhaps he is changing still, although what form— I see that your light is changing.

Ornatus: For some reason I find the story disturbing. It is as if—well, it doesn't matter.

Sidonia: As if the city could no longer protect us?

Ornatus: That would be blasphemy.

Sidonia: No. After all, we are some distance away. But we should go back. I can see that you are anxious.

Ornatus: Yes. We ought to return.

Sidonia: And then Plato can entertain us with some more of his ancient words.

9

remote control: a form of worship conducted by the people of Mouldwarp, in the belief that they might manipulate distant events with certain ritualised ceremonies. Tribal dancing may have been part of these rites, but it is also likely that letters or numbers were chanted as a way of summoning the mechanical spirits of the earth.

rock music: the sound of old stones. This is a condition not previously ascribed to Mouldwarp, but the phrase itself is evidence that some connection was made between ancient objects and musical harmony.

second in command: the belief in the supremacy of time. All aspects of existence were once governed by this concept, as in second sight, second thoughts and second childhood.

see red: to see into the fire at the heart of all things.

sexist: a proponent of the notion that there were only two or, at most, three sexes.

sleeping car: an example of the belief that inanimate objects, when not being employed or exploited, reverted to a dormant state. See 'sleeping bag' and 'sleeping tablet'.

solitary confinement: a state of mind, much encouraged in the Mouldwarp period.

space age: the space between objects was believed to grow old and die; it was a way of assigning mortality, and fatality, to the entire universe.

stopwatch: a group of trained observers chosen to measure the pace of human affairs and to intervene if there were any signs of delay. There seems to have been a general delight in speed and efficiency for their own sake, with the attendant fear that the world might lose its velocity or even stop altogether.

sunstroke: the death of the sun.

telepathy: the suffering caused by 'television'. It seems likely that television enlarged the organs of vision beyond their natural range and as a result caused mental distress. Efforts were continually being made to increase human perception by artificial means, without any understanding that the conditions of Mouldwarp were still in place—the greater the enlargement, in fact, the more obvious the constriction. The practitioners of television received magnified images of their own shrunken sight and lived in perpetual sorrow.

third world: unknown. The home of the third person? Hence the location known as the third degree? Doubtful.

time bomb: the explosion of the Mouldwarp world.

tin god: an object of their worship.

town crier: an official who took on the woes of a town, or district, and engaged in ritual weeping to ensure the maintenance of harmony.

transcendence or *trans-end-dance*: the ability to move beyond the end, otherwise called the dance of death. The fear of death, in the Mouldwarp period, was part of a greater fear of life.

travel sickness: the fever which prevented certain people from leaving the sites of their birth or upbringing. It is now known to be a sacred condition created by the earth itself, but in ancient times it was classified as an illness to be purged with drugs.

underground: the title of a painting of great beauty. It is before you now. Notice how the blue and red lines of light reach out in wonderful curves and ovals, while a great yellow circle completes the design. It is a masterpiece of formal fluency and, although the people of Mouldwarp are considered to be devoid of spiritual genius, there are some who believe this to be their sacred symbol of harmony. It is true that certain spirit names have been deciphered—angel, temple, white city, gospel oak and the legendary seven sisters—but the central purpose of the painting is still disputed.

wisdom teeth: it was believed that the source of human characteristics or behaviour could be found in various organs of the body. Courage was identified with the heart, for example, and memory with the brain. It would seem, then, that wisdom was located in the teeth.

word processor: in the old machine culture words were seen as commodities, or items in a line of production. They became a form of manufacture and were, therefore, increasingly standardised; they took on mechanical rather than living proportions, so that they could be widely distributed over the world.

words-worth: the patronymic of writers who had earned their high position. In a similar context we have Chatter-ton. Many Mouldwarp writers were compared to inorganic substances, such as Ore-well, Cole-ridge and Gold-smith. Some writers were considered sacred, as in Pope and Priestley. Some were feared as Wilde or Savage while others were celebrated for their mournful or querulous style, among them Graves, Bellow and Frost. Unfortunately, no specimens of their work have survived.

X-ray: a ray that has dissolved or has been terminated. X, also known as 'the cross', was a symbol of great power in the Age of Mouldwarp; it was widely used to indicate death, as in X-am or X-it.

yellow fever: the fear of colour.

zero tolerance: the ability to exist in a world without numbers. Since in this period there was no reality beyond the numerical system, it was regarded as an infinitely remote theoretical possibility.

zoolog:

I am being interrupted.

IO

Apologies, Plato. We have recovered some images from the marshland of the Savoy: powder upon a face, a glass of liquid, a child, a white bar of cleansing ointment, a vehicle upon wheels, a perfume for the hair, a shirt for the male, a basin. We cannot be certain how these details are related.

Thank you. I will consider these matters before my next oration.

II

Very little is known of that ancient race, the American people. Their territory is now a vast and featureless desert, according to the latest report, swept by gales of hot air. Yet we have discovered evidence that, beneath the surface of this wasteland, there may remain the vestiges of a great empire. A sealed casket was removed from the ruined circus of Eros, outside our own walls; it was of course considered to be a sacred object, and lay untouched for several hundred years. But then, after the inauguration of our own Academy of Past Ages, it was removed for examination. The casket itself had been fashioned from some unknown metallic substance, and on its side it bore the still faintly discernible legend 'E. A. Poe. American. 1809–1849'; when it was opened it was found to contain a text of black type inscribed 'Tales and Histories'. It was a wonderful revelation, since it was the first relic of that unknown civilisation; unfortunately it is also likely to be the last. If all the earth were glass, as the saying goes, we would still look in vain. The significance of 'Tales and Histories' is immense, therefore, as the unique record of a lost race.

The eminence and status of the author are not in doubt. The name, for example, was not difficult to interpret. Poe is an abbreviation of Poet, and by common consent the rest was deciphered: E. A. Poe = Eminent American Poet. It seems clear enough that the writers of America enjoyed a blessed anonymity, even in the Age of Mouldwarp. The word 'poet' is known to all of us, but as there are no chants or hymns in 'Tales and Histories' we believe the term was applied indiscriminately to all writers of that civilisation. This particular text has been preserved because of its historical content, not because it was the material for song and dance.

Certainly E. A. Poet has described the characteristics of the American empire with great precision. Its inhabitants dwelled in very large and very old houses which, perhaps because of climatic conditions, were often covered with lichen or ivy. In many respects the architecture of these ancient mansions conformed to the same pattern; they contained libraries and galleries, chambers of antique painting and long corridors leading in serpentine fashion to great bolted doors. Their rooms were characteristically large and lofty, with narrow pointed windows and dark floors of the wood named 'oak'. They also included innumerable staircases and cellars; the passages were lit by candelabra, although it was customary for the owner of the house to carry a flaming torch when walking upstairs. One eminent family, the Ushers, were fortunate enough to possess vaults in which they could bury their dead without the inconvenience of a church service. Indeed from the evidence of the Poet, the American people had no established or organised religion; they seem to have possessed a great terror of the night and darkness, like many primitive races, but there was an evil deity which they chose to propitiate with elaborate ceremonies and rituals. In one of the Poet's historical accounts we find a reference to the 'palace of the fiend, Gin'; this of course is related to Ijin, who, in the stories of the eastern earth, is an imp or demon. We have discovered the name of an essay by the Poet, 'The Imp of the Perverse', which was no doubt a catechism or devotional study. On occasions such as this we recognise, with some distress, how much has been lost to us.

The greatest fear of the Americans, however, seems

to have been that of premature burial. This anxiety was related to the superstition, known as Cry-o-gene, which taught that the soul could be trapped within the confines of its body by lowering its temperature; it was believed that the frozen spirit could not fly out of its nest. No. There is no cause for laughter. The landscape of America was monotonous and forbidding; its seasons of cold were prolonged beyond endurance and there was more 'night' than 'day'.

This may account, in certain respects, for the striking appearance of its inhabitants. The Americans had pale countenances, with thin lips and large eyes; their hair was generally long and silken. It seems likely, from the evidence of this history, that they were all of distant aristocratic lineage; one of our readers has suggested that they were descended from some original clan or household, which might account for their marked and peculiar characteristics. We are informed by the learned Poet that they were a highly nervous people, who suffered from a morbid acuteness of their faculties. They experienced continually 'a vague feeling of terror and despair'. They were prone to the most extreme sensations of wonder or hilarity and there seems to have been an unusual amount of lunacy among the young.

Their fear of premature burial has already been discussed, but it was accompanied by a sense of sin and evil so strong that many believed that they were already damned. All the thoughts of Americans were upon death. Why such a wealthy and aristocratic people should have been so susceptible to morbid dread, and why they chose to live among so many intimations of gloom and decay, are still questions to be resolved. It has been suggested that they suffered from some general and inherited disease that caused them to shrink from bright light, for example, and that kept them enclosed within their mansions. But there may be another explanation.

May I quote from the Poet's own words? 'And then, after the lapse of sixty minutes (which embrace three thousand and six hundred seconds of the Time that flies), there came yet another chiming of the clock and then were the same disconcert and tremulousness and meditation as before.' Some of you are bewildered. A 'clock' was a mechanical system that manufactured this 'Time'. There may originally have been covered markets from which Time was distributed to the people but, in the period when the Poet wrote his history, the mechanisms were so compact that it could be produced by means of various wheels and dials. There is also mentioned, within the same account, the object known as a 'pendulum' attached to this clock. There is even a 'pit' where Time itself was stored.

All the evidence, therefore, suggests that the Americans considered Time to be an indispensable element of their existence. There is in the text a toast or homage to this deity, with the refrain 'Time, gentlemen, please'. It was also, perhaps, a visible being. I have already mentioned that the Poet writes of 'the Time that flies', which suggests that they saw winged or hastening figures; this may also explain the references, on several occasions, to 'muffled' or 'low indefinite sounds', which we interpret as the noise of footsteps or of beating wings. But at this point we confess ourselves to be intrigued by that passage describing the 'disconcert and tremulousness and meditation' which Time instilled within the people. They trembled in its presence and as it 'flew' it gave them cause for anxious contemplation. But even though it was by no means a beneficent agency, they believed that it was in some obscure sense part of their own bodies. The beating of the human heart, for example, is compared to such sounds as 'a watch makes when enveloped in cotton'. A 'watch' was that part of the clock which stared at its owner, and was sometimes known as its 'face'.

Another paragraph in 'Tales and Histories' anticipates the discoveries of a much later period. After the mansions of the American people have been described, it is suggested that these splendid houses 'moulded the destinies' of those who inhabited them; they contained 'an atmosphere peculiar to themselves' which wielded 'an importunate and terrible influence' upon those who dwelled in them. Curious, is it not? This historian of ancient days might easily be mistaken for a prophet! But then we read this: 'I am heartily sick of this life and of the nineteenth century in general. I am convinced that everything is going wrong.' Ponder these words, which manifest such a great sense of woe and loss. The conclusion is more poignant still. 'I will get embalmed for a couple of hundred years.' There of course is the pathos and also the irony. If the Poet were indeed revived, two hundred years later, the Age of Mouldwarp would still be in existence with all its degraded power. But although it was a barren and oppressive epoch, the work before us confirms that even then there were intimations and gleams of another life which would eventually emerge within the great brightness of Witspell. Thank you.

12

Plato: Thank you. Something of a success, I think.

Soul: It was a fine performance.

Plato: But was it accurate?

Soul: As far as anyone knows. I particularly enjoyed your disquisition on time. It always interested me, at least when it existed. You were very convincing, too. And I must say that your gestures have improved.

Plato: I was taught in the Academy how to summon up the images, but I was a poor student.

Soul: No. You were different. I noticed it from the

beginning. Even as a child you were unlike the others. You preferred solitude. You refused to play with the broken mirrors.

Plato: I was so ugly—

Soul: No. You were so afraid. When you were supposed to dance in the maze with the other children, you screamed and ran away.

Plato: I did?

Soul: I was always with you. When you used to hide in the ruins of the elephantine castle. When you wept at the death of your teacher.

Plato: Euphrene. She brought me into the Academy. She showed me the books.

Soul: Do you remember weeping?

Plato: I remember that I visited the House of the Dead.

13

Welcome, little Plato. Welcome to the House of the Dead. When your teacher approached her end, she came here. Some citizens gently and quietly disappear, while others will lie within their shells for many centuries before fading away. We had once thought that, at the moment of death, all memory and imagination left the body; but recently we have found evidence that there is dreaming among the dead. They lie here and dream of their past lives. We know this because we have listened to their dreams. Why are you weeping, little Plato?

14

Soul: Yet you stayed at the Academy.

Plato: It was my duty. No. It was my choice. I wanted to read all the old books. I was no longer here. I was there, within them.

Soul: It was a comfortable position.

Plato: Why?

Soul: It was a place where you could conceal yourself.

Plato: You're wrong.

Soul: I ought to know.

Plato: I wanted to find myself.

Soul: You wanted to find a voice.

Plato: No. I wanted to find a faith.

Soul: It was all very distressing. You were certain that you were right and the other citizens wrong. You believed in the importance of the past.

Plato: Of course. But surely it was you who convinced me that the books were worthy of examination?

Soul: I may have done. I cannot remember.

Plato: Souls do not need memory. They are eternal.

Soul: My apologies. I stand corrected. But when they asked you to take on the robe of orator, I remained silent.

Plato: That was my choice. I did it because I was afraid.

Soul: Of what?

Plato: Of them.

15

*Plato of Pie Corner, you have assumed the robe and mask of
the orator. You will speak at each of the gates of the city.
What is your theme?*

I will discuss the first ages of the earth.

16

The Age of Orpheus is the name we have given to the first epoch, when it was truly the springtime of this world. These were the centuries when statues were coaxed into life and walked from their stone plinths, when the spirits of streams could be changed into trees or glades and when flowers sprang from the blood of wounded heroes. The gods themselves took the shape of swans or bulls from the simple delight in transformation.

Orpheus has become the symbol of this enchanted

time because it was he who discovered the powers of musical harmony and, by means of his melodies, made the trees dance and the mountains speak. Yet his delight in the plaintive notes of the lute was far exceeded by his love for a woman, Eurydice, who was the daughter of a river nymph; we have found the nests of nymphs even here, by the Tyburn and the Lea. Eurydice was stung by a serpent of the field while conversing with a flower; she died at once, her eyes closed upon the world, and Orpheus was afflicted with a grief which no music could alleviate. We might say that he 'descended' into grief, since the notion of descent is central to the vision of this age.

She herself had been transformed into a shade and taken to the place known as Hades, a dark subterranean city of which certain ruined fragments have already been found. Its ruler was Thanatos, the son of Chronos, which is to say that death is the child of time. He wore a black gown upon which were woven golden stars, as a sign that the heavens themselves were in turn the creation of time and death.

So piercing was Orpheus's sorrow at the loss of Eurydice that he approached the gods of Mount Olympus, situated in Asia Minor, and implored them to grant his wish. Could he travel to the underworld and see her once more? He was warned that any journey beneath the earth would be perilous indeed but, after some discussion over bowls of ambrosia, the gods allowed him to venture below. Almost at once he

51

was transported to the mouth of the cavern; he was about to enter, when a ferocious three-headed dog came towards him out of the darkness. (The bones of a grotesque animal have indeed been found near the site of the ruined city.) Orpheus had no sense of fear, however, and began to play upon his lute; the monstrous dog stopped, licked its paws with its three tongues and settled comfortably upon the floor of the cave. Then it fell asleep. As soon as he heard it snoring and whimpering, Orpheus slipped past and entered the domain of Hades.

In fact the echo of his music had preceded his arrival, and it is said that the shadowy inhabitants of this place had suspended their labours in order to listen to the strange sweetness of the sounds. So he was greeted with soft sighs before being taken to the palace of Thanatos himself. He was escorted through various rooms hung with dismal tapestries until he reached a dark and secluded chamber, where the ruler reclined on a couch of black marble. Orpheus knelt before him and, having announced his mission, again played upon his lute. Thanatos was ravished by the music and, wiping away his ruby tears, graciously agreed that Orpheus might reclaim Eurydice and lead her upwards.

Before this reunion, however, he decided that his guest must see the wonders of the city. He showed him a wheel of fire, always turning, and a great stone that rolled backwards and forwards along the same course. There was also a river of salt water, encircling the region, that forever turned upon itself. These were of course the old emblems of time. Thanatos imposed one condition upon the release of Eurydice: Orpheus was not to look upon her until they had left Hades and reached the outer air. The reasons for his decision are unclear and no state papers have yet been recovered, but it is likely that the sudden immersion within the realm of time had somehow disfigured or even transformed her.

So Orpheus turned his back and, staying true to his oath, began walking ahead of Eurydice towards the light; he stayed upon the straight path, between vast walls of dark rock and played upon his lute in order to encourage her faltering steps. But there came a moment when he could not resist the comfort of her face and, without thought, he turned his head and gazed upon her. It was already too late. She cried aloud, and fell back in a faint. Orpheus ran towards her, but she had faded away before he could reach her outstretched arms. He heard only the faintest echo of 'Farewell' before he found himself alone upon the stony path. Alone he reached the territory of light.

It has been said that Eurydice did not wish to leave the world of time and deliberately called out to him so that he would look at her; she had grown old, perhaps, and did not believe that he would love her in her altered state. The truth has yet to be discovered. Orpheus himself wandered among the fields and meadows of his native land, always lamenting, until the gods took pity on him. He was lifted into the heavens, where his lute was changed into a constellation; from that period onward, the people of the earth could hear the music of the spheres.

It is in many respects a poignant story, but there is no reason to doubt its general truth. Although certain details have yet to be authenticated the existence of Hades and Mount Olympus, as well as the star cluster of Lyra, has already been proved. In the sad fate of Orpheus, then, we have a central and genuine event of ancient history. You may now enter the observation chamber, where the three-headed dog has been reconstructed, before I begin a brief exequy on the second age of the earth.

17

The Age of the Apostles was an age of suffering and lamentation, when the earth itself was considered to be evil and all those upon it were condemned as sinners. The gods had departed and it was believed that the natural world had betrayed its spiritual inheritance. The apostles propagated a doctrine that the human race had committed some terrible offence, of unknown origin, which could only be expiated by prayer and penance; it was not long, in fact, before pain was valued for its own sake. They also insisted that the various gods had become one deity, which hid itself in a cloud or, on occasions, in a bright light. This god, according to the testimony of the apostles, had already consigned some of its creatures to everlasting torment in a region known as hell; its location has not yet been found, but we believe it to lie in a territory adjacent to Hades. We are certain, however, that the religion of the apostles was indeed one of blood and sorrow. That is why, in this ancient period, the angels rarely visited the earth; if they alighted here they stayed only for a moment since, as Gabriel himself has told us, there was no chance of intelligent conversation.

The reasons for the eventual collapse of the religion are unknown, although it is likely that certain internal contradictions rendered it unstable. It affirmed the values of compassion and sympathy, for example, while persecuting those who refused to accept its authority; it worshipped an omnipotent deity, while insisting upon the individual's free choice of salvation or damnation. These paradoxes were maintained for many centuries but in the end the faith collapsed and gave way to the apparently more plausible explanations of Mouldwarp.

I 8

Plato: I was so delighted that I could speak without faltering.

Soul: As I was saying before you interrupted me, you had found your voice.

Plato: And the citizens have been pleased by it. It is almost as if I am protecting them at the same time as I am protecting myself. As long as I study and interpret the past, they are able to ignore it. I give them certainty and that is enough.

Soul: But they listen very intently.

Plato: And they laugh.

Soul: No. You misunderstand them. They are simply admiring your skills as an orator. Do you recall your description of the last days of Mouldwarp? That was a grand performance.

19

The last centuries of Mouldwarp furnish perhaps the most solemn and awful scenes in the entire history of the earth. Who can properly depict, for example, the despair engendered by the cult of webs and nets which spread among the people in these final years? They seem to have worn these dismal garments as a form of enslavement as well as worship, as if their own darkness might thereby be covered and concealed. They had inherited the superstition of progress from their credulous ancestors but in their extremity they had no notion of what, if anything, they were progressing towards. Nothing could have prepared them, however, for the horror of the end.

The priests of this age had lost their visionary powers and had become technicians; so restricted was the range of their knowledge that their principal activity lay in the computation of figures and numbers within the material world. One group of this priestly caste had been trained to observe the heavens (according to the ancient texts they were known as astronomads or, perhaps, astronumberers) in order to confirm the regularity and predictability of its movements. We believe this to have been known as science. Yet there came a moment when one observer noticed that certain faint sources of light had somehow disappeared. An observer in a different region confirmed that other remote areas of brightness had also vanished. In their anxiety and alarm the astronumberers consulted together, only to realise that these stars and nebulae had disappeared simply because no one had been looking at them. With increasing desperation the technicians consulted their maps and their models in order to compile a list of celestial objects that had not been under continuous observation. Of course these objects had also gone. The leaders of Mouldwarp were suddenly confronted by the knowledge that the components of their universe ceased to exist when they were not actively sought or studied. Within a generation there emerged a common belief that the night sky, and all of its properties, had been created by human perception.

Every galaxy and every constellation then became the object of continual attention, as if it were still possible to keep this universe together by an act of concerted will. But it was already too late. They had begun to doubt. Then all the stars, quadrant by quadrant, were gradually extinguished. Once the process had begun, it could not be halted; the onset of decay in one section of the heavens spread across the entire night sky. Since the astronomads now believed that they were responsible for what they observed, they could no longer define their objectives with any confidence or certainty. And so the darkness spread.

The populace had not been informed of these events and had not noticed the disappearance of a few distant stars. But when the most prominent patterns of the night sky were slowly eroded, there emerged a great and consuming fear. It was suggested that they should pray. Pray? To what? Long ago they had forsaken any idea of divinity within, or beyond, themselves. Who can imagine the scenes of fury and despair when the work of Mouldwarp began to unravel after eight hundred years? The anger of the people was first directed against the priests who had apparently deceived and manipulated them; they turned upon those who had created reason and abstraction and the encroaching darkness. But the practitioners of science were themselves horrified and bewildered by the events unfolding above them. They had never understood that they were engaged in acts of magic, and that their universe was an emanation of the human mind. Then the sun went out.

The ensuing period of anger and fear has often been chronicled. The people of Mouldwarp did not, or could not, recognise the light within themselves; so they raged against the dark and the false reality that had been constructed around them. Some wondered how they still lived and breathed, but most of the inhabitants of this lost civilisation were provoked into bouts of violence and destruction. They turned first against the engines of their masters and, according to our historians, began the burning of the machines. In the general conflagration they set alight the nets and webs which had been the garments of their superstitious cult, and broke apart all the screens and signs by which it had been organised. Once they had lost control of their universe, they lost faith in the civilisation that had created it. Their computational tools, their forms of communication, their modes of transport, all seemed irrelevant and inconsequential in the night that now enshrouded their world. So they finished with them. They destroyed them. They burned them to the ground. Only then, in the exhaustion and silent despair which marked the demise of Mouldwarp, did the light of humankind begin its ministry.

Soon after the general conflagration, when the fires subsided, a subdued and dusky light seemed to emerge from the earth itself and grew in strength as it enveloped the people. Eventually there was broad day, without that night sky which had for so long deluded and controlled them; they rejoiced, but then became afraid when they realised that the light also came from within themselves. This was the moment when we can, with some certainty, date the opening of Witspell.

20

Plato: I offered the citizens such certainty that they had no need to enquire for themselves. I, too, was so certain. Was I right?

Soul: I cannot say.

Plato: What if the past is all invention or legend?

Soul: It is unlikely.

Plato: Let me put it differently, then. What if my interpretation of the books is false or misguided?

Soul: Who would ever know?

Plato: You would.

Soul: I know what you know.

Plato: For an immortal being, you are very modest. You understand the past, after all, and you can see into the future.

Soul: Perhaps they are the same thing.

Plato: In the Age of Witspell the people were informed that future events affected every aspect of their present.

Soul: So you believe.

Plato: So I believed. Did I mention it in my oration?

21

The Age of Witspell emerged when human light began to appear upon the earth. The darkness of Mouldwarp was dispersed and the citizens recognised one another without fear or dissembling. But if this early time was filled with exhilaration and awakening, it was also marked by unhappiness and difficulty for those who were afraid of their own freedom. There were some who believed that this new world existed only within their own minds, for example, and they fled from each other, howling. Others closed their eyes upon it and slept for ever.

But the age of anxiety passed, together with the illusions of abstract law and uniform dimensions. The first evidence of change came when it was reported that a centaur had been seen galloping across the meadows of Greece. This was followed by the news that a phoenix had been observed rising from its ashes somewhere in northern France; it was approximately the size of an eagle, with feathers of purple and gold. When sirens were heard off the coast of Asia Minor, as well as banshee keening outside Dublin, it became clear that the manifold spirits of the earth had crept from their confinement of almost a thousand years. There were stories of elves and kraken, sylphs and valkyries, unicorns and salamanders; the fabric of the old reality had dissolved or, rather, it had become interwoven with so many others that it could only rarely be glimpsed.

How otherwise can we understand the legends of early Witspell? We read of great golden ships sailing from El Dorado with cargoes of golden fruit and monkeys with gold-flecked fur, and of envoys from Utopia who had been wandering for many centuries before finding harbour in London. This was the period when Atlantis, otherwise known as Avalon or Cockaigne or the Isle of the Blessed, emerged from the ocean; it had always lain beneath the surface of Mouldwarp vision, but now it rose in glory. There were less consoling prospects, however, when the pit of Maleborge was discovered in Sumatra and a Slough of Despond located on the border of Wales.

But nothing could affect the enthusiasm of our ancestors when they discovered the history of their own city. From the writings of that great scholar and historian Geoffrey of Monmouth they learned that London had been founded by Brutus of Troy at the time when 'the Ark of the Covenant was taken by the Philistines'. Other writers of record have been discovered—the names of Macaulay and Trevelyan are among them—but they are of a later date and therefore less reliable. From Monmouth the citizens of Witspell discovered that, after the fall of Troy, Brutus was greeted in vision by the goddess Diana; she commanded him to sail to an island beyond the setting of his sun, and establish a city which would become the wonder of the world. This island was known as Albion and after Brutus had landed upon its white shore he encountered a race of giants whom eventually he overcame in battle. We have found evidence for those giants, of course, in the great hills that still surround us; the remains of their burial chambers can be seen in the museum of silence. After his victory Brutus established the city of New Troy, later known as Lud's Town or London, and bequeathed to it a code of spiritual law which continued through the reigns of Lear, Cordelia and Lud himself. No other monarchs are known to us, although Macaulay and Trevelyan have created fanciful dynasties which can safely be consigned to the dark world of Mouldwarp theory from which they came.

A great figure has been raised from the fields of Finsbury, where it had lain unknown for many centuries; the quality of its stonework places it in the middle period of Witspell, and there is evidence of a ritual avenue or cursus encircling it. Samples of the ground have been examined, from which we conclude that this statue was surrounded by monumental candles that rose into the upper air; they were set afire, perhaps, with lightning created by some unknown agency. The arms of the figure are raised, as if in greeting or celebration, while between her breasts are inscribed the letters LO; a more remarkable device is to be found on her stomach, however, where a large circle has been carved. Within this circle are patterns of intricate lines, which on closer inspection reveal themselves to be the avenues and dwellings of London; one gentle curve imitates that of the Thames. The significance of LO then became obvious to us. This exalted, even sublime, figure was a sacred representation of the city itself! We suggest, therefore, that the citizens venerated London as a living god. It is possible that they also offered sacrifices to it, but of this we cannot be certain.

The worship of London would, in turn, account for certain other suggestive aspects of Witspell. The ancient tribal trackways around the city were restored or, as our ancestors put it, 'reawakened'. We read that buildings became flowers, and flowers buildings, but the meaning is unclear. The burial rites are also significant, since the citizens were interred in precisely the same attitude as the monumental statue—arms held aloft, with the letters LO and the image of London painted upon the bodies. Could it be that in death they had become part of the divine city, or did London itself manifest the general spiritual will and being of its inhabitants? The odour of sweet herbs and incense was always noticeable when the tombs were opened, and each body had a golden band around its forehead. Those who had survived the catastrophe of Mouldwarp, and had first created human light, knew that they were blessed. So, as a historian of the period has remarked, when the people of Witspell buried one of their number they believed that they were burying a god.

22

Sparkler: The children are always eager to listen to him. Do you see the way they flock towards him when he appears?

Madrigal: Only because he is as small as they are. Yet soon enough they will reach the age when they must paint their features upon the Wall. Do you recall when you and I and Plato took our sticks of coloured light and traced our outlines upon the stones?

Sparkler: Did Sidonia paint herself holding a lamp?

Madrigal: I cannot remember. But I do recall that she erased some of her face. Yet, even so, everyone could tell by her features from what parish she came.

Sparkler: And then Plato depicted himself wearing the cap of feathers—

Madrigal: The cap of the city fool.

Sparkler: And holding out a script of glass.

Madrigal: He might have been anticipating his own fate.

Sparkler: Or, as he would say, his fate had happened already.

Madrigal: That is precisely the kind of thing he tells the children. Oh, there is the daughter of Ornatus. Look. She is laughing. No doubt Plato is talking once more about Mouldwarp.

Sparkler: But where is the humour in these ancient practices? Truly, they make me shudder.

Madrigal: You have to admit that they have their funny side. Who would have thought, for example, that our ancestors would look upwards for guidance?

Sparkler: Ridiculous. Was that in Mouldwarp or in Witspell?

Madrigal: Mouldwarp, I think. It is all rather confusing.

Ornatus: Sparkler and Madrigal, hail and farewell.

Madrigal: Where are you going in such a hurry? To meet your daughter?

Ornatus: Plato has chosen a new theme. He is about to begin at the clerk's well.

Sparkler: Unfortunately, Ornatus, we are both a little tired. We will have to rely upon you for a report.

23

We have acquired some information about the actors and comedians of past ages, but our knowledge has been greatly increased by the chance survival of a comic handbook entitled *Jokes and Their Relation to the Unconscious*. The meaning of 'unconscious' is by no means clear, but it may be related to the idea of drunkenness, which even in our own time is the object of laughter. The joke book itself is the work of a clown or buffoon who was billed as Sigmund Freud—no doubt pronounced 'Fraud' to add piquancy to his stage character. In this volume he has compiled examples of what he calls 'significant nonsense', with comic routines concerning people who forget names or misread words, who use the wrong set of keys or knock over pots of black dye. Clearly Freud himself was an incomparable gamester, and it is easy to imagine him reciting these absurd misadventures with a serious face.

His act would have been described as 'smutty' or 'bringing out the blue bag' and, with its emphasis upon sex, it was a well-known aspect of the primitive theatre. His 'lingo' was in turn based upon the confrontation between audience and performer, with the continual use of Freud's famous catchphrase—'I think I should be the judge of that!'—as the signal for more laughter.

But the most hilarious examples of Freudian repartee took place when his partner, Oedipus, appeared on the stage. This 'fall guy' or 'straight man' may have been some relic of the old pantomimic tradition, since he wore loose white robes and displayed that glum expression characteristic of the pantaloon. He also adopted a peculiarly rapid and sliding walk known to devotees as 'the Freudian slip'. He would try unsuccessfully to use it every time Freud began to question or 'analyse' him with a number of delightfully absurd questions.

'Are you repressing something, Oedipus?'

'Of course not. I am standing very upright, as the soldier said to the nursemaid.'

'Now now, Pussy. None of your nonsense here. Tell me, what is your opinion of chair legs and train tunnels?'

'Rather out than in, as the bishop—'

'I think, Puss, you are beginning to prove my point.'

'Don't talk to me about points. Not after last night.'

'How do you feel about long noses?'

'I've never felt one in my life!'

'Come now. That's no answer to one of my famous analytical questions.'

'Well then, Sigmund, I will tell you the honest truth. I think that they should be blown.'

'Oedipus, you must have been a very funny child.'

'Funny? I had them screaming. Especially mother.'

This dialogue known as 'chaff' or 'patter' must have reduced the Mouldwarp audience to tears of laughter, especially when Freud steps forward to inform them that 'it is all the fault of my friend's unconscious'—i.e. that he is drunk.

It has often been noted that the people of Mould-warp were preoccupied with sexual activity at the expense of all other principles of life; there is even some evidence to suggest that they identified themselves in terms of their sexual orientation. No. There is no cause for embarrassment. Our purpose is to understand, not to lay blame.

Nevertheless, despite—or even because of—their obsession with sexual practice it is likely that they laughed as heartily at Freud's antics as we do. We salute him, therefore, as a great comic genius of his age.

24

Sidonia: Have I interrupted your recital, Plato?

Plato: No. Not at all. I have ended with a flourish.

Sidonia: I wanted you to be the first to hear the wonderful news.

Plato: Oh? What is it?

Sidonia: A great pole has been found at the corner of Lime Street and Leadenhall. It came out of the earth so quietly and quickly that it might not have been buried at all.

Plato: If it was found at the corner of Leadenhall,

then it must be the great maypole that stood on the site for many hundreds of years. It was the centre of our city's festivity and celebration.

Sidonia: And there are words upon it, partly defaced but still visible. I noted them down.

Plato: What is this? 'Ove Arup and Partners. For the Lloyd's Building.'

Sidonia: I admit that I was puzzled. That is why I came to you.

Plato: If it is in the same location, then it must be the maypole. Everything in our city's history tells us that the first and original shape never dies.

Sidonia: So?

Plato: The Lloyd's Building must have been the name given to the maypole. Ove and Arup and Partners were the deities guarding it.

Sidonia: Can that be true?

Plato: There can be no doubt.

25

Plato: There can be no doubt. Can there?

Soul: It's no good asking me. I have nothing to do with knowledge, certain or uncertain. I am all love and intuition.

Plato: If you love me, then you will tell me. Can I be sure of what I say? Sometimes I feel that it is all pretence, and that I should take doubt like a dagger and plunge it into me. When I am wounded, then I might speak the truth.

Soul: Ouch.

Plato: You think I am being extravagant?

Soul: I take the long view in such matters. Whatever is good for you is right.

Plato: But surely you understand? You are the one who gave me my restlessness. My nervous fear.

Soul: Why should I be blamed? You are what you are. I am part of you, I admit it, but I really cannot bear all the responsibility.

Plato: So you are ashamed of me.

Soul: Not at all. I do not always enjoy your arguments, but I find them necessary. When you give expression to your thoughts, you help to define me. Is that selfish?

Plato: We were taught that the pattern of birds in flight was also an image of their soul. I suppose that you and I bear the same relationship.

Soul: And we, too, are part of the soul of the world. Then beyond that—well, it becomes more mysterious.

Plato: So you will never leave me?

Soul: A body without a soul is an impossibility, although I admit that there are times when I long to 'sup above'. But of course I would never deprive you of your—how shall I put it?—your spirit.

Plato: Thank you. You lend me courage.

Soul: It is not a loan. It is a gift. You may need it soon.

Plato: You intrigue me.

Soul: Hush. Look into your heart now and speak to the citizens about the wonders of creation.

26

The ancient myths of creation are of the utmost interest to those of us who study the poetry of past ages. It was believed, for example, that a god called Khnumu fashioned a great egg in which all of creation resided; another deity, Ptal, then broke the egg with a hammer and life spilled out. This was known as the 'big bang', from which the universe was supposed continually to expand. Of course the poets of creation did not realise that what they considered to be flying outwards was, in reality, the retreat or recession of their own divine energy. They had, as it were, taken a hammer to their own brains.

From an ancient city named Babylon we have evidence of a creation song which is altogether more convincing. The two forces of light and darkness, otherwise called god and dragon, fight for mastery; god slays the dragon, but even in his death agonies darkness is able to sow the seeds of confusion in an otherwise enlightened universe. This was 'chaos theory', in which the dragon's mouth became known as a black hole or, in another myth, dark matter. Such legendary creatures as the white dwarf and the brown dwarf also appear in these wonderful sagas. Their central purpose has, perhaps, become clear to you? The singers and prophets of antiquity had such little faith in their own powers that they felt compelled to invoke some great and distant source from which they had come. The knowledge that everything, past and future alike, exists eternally—this was not given to them.

That very interesting mythographer, Mennocchio, suggested that the four elements of the early myths—earth, air, fire and water—were once congealed together in a mass of putrefaction; that the worms who burrowed through it were the angels, and that one of those angels became God. This became known as the 'wormhole theory', which prompted much elaborate speculation. It was exceeded in inventiveness only by the story of 'superstrings', which can be tentatively dated to the civilisation that first propounded the music of the spheres. These 'strings' also appeared in other myths which emphasised the role of harmony and symmetry in the creation of the universe. When such fables were recited to the populace, we may imagine the ritual accompaniment of many instruments. It may seem peculiar to us that our earliest ancestors always looked back to some mythical point of origin, but no doubt our own speculations would have puzzled them. We now realise that creation occurs continually. We are creation. We are the music.

27

Waiter: Welcome to the museum of noise, sirs. What do you lack?

Madrigal: What do I lack?

Sparkler: That was the way people talked. He is asking whether you would prefer wine or coffee.

Madrigal: Why does he want to give me wine and coffee?

Sparkler: This is meant to be a coffee-house. It is the custom. Of course you are expected to pay for it.

Madrigal: Who does he think he is?

Waiter: Please, citizens, what is it that you lack?

Madrigal: Yes. I lack a sense of place. Where are we supposed to be?

Waiter: On the corner of Lombard Street. Just before the Mansion House.

Madrigal: There is no noise at all. We might as well be in the museum of silence.

Sparkler: Hush. Can you hear that footstep? Like a heartbeat? Now you can sense the sound of more steps against the stone. Others are joining them.

Madrigal: They are becoming too loud.

Sparkler: They are the steps of countless generations.

Madrigal: Now they grow low and remote.

Sparkler: It is evening time. Can you hear laughter and conversation at the other tables? And the noises from the kitchen below?

Madrigal: Is it all real?

Sparkler: That is not a question anyone can answer.

Madrigal: I believe that I will have wine, after all. What do you call the young attendant?

Sparkler: Waiter.

Madrigal: Waiter! I will pay for wine!

Sparkler: Good. And now you can tell me about Plato's oration on Penton Hill.

Madrigal: Were you not there?

Sparkler: No. I had been chosen to work.

Madrigal: Congratulations!

Sparkler: I was fortunate. But I was sorry to have missed the performance. How did it begin?

Madrigal: This seat of wood is very hard.

Sparkler: It will help you to concentrate. Tell me what Plato said.

28

Approximately six hundred years ago a long strip of images, embossed upon some pliable material, was discovered among the ruins of the south bank; they became visible when held in the light, which caused some historians to suggest that they were a form of palpable or concentrated luminescence. Two words have been reconstructed, 'Hitchcock' and 'Frenzy', but the nature and purpose of the strip are still unclear. We have lit the images in various ways; we have moved them in several directions, and at different speeds, but their meaning remains mysterious.

Even in its incomplete state, however, 'Hitchcock Frenzy' is a magnificent discovery, since we soon recognised that the images themselves were representations of Mouldwarp London. Imagine our surprise when we saw the ancient people hastening down their lighted pathways and engaged in ritual action! The first picture was of a stone bridge with a dark tower upon each bank. Surely the river beneath it was too narrow and turbulent to be the beloved Thames? But then her familiar tidal pattern was noticed. This was our river, after all, yet one filled with shadows and pools of darkness.

There are even more extraordinary scenes when it becomes clear that a creature or person is diving and swooping above the river. It cannot be seen, but it sees all. It sees tall buildings and lighted rooms; it sees streets and faces; it sees strange grey birds and small boats upon the water. It rises and falls, gliding invisibly through the London air. Could it be some high priestess, called Hitchcock Frenzy? We have no knowledge, however, of astral magic in the Age of Mouldwarp. It has been suggested that it is the work of an angel, who excreted the material strip of light while flying over the city, but there has been no confirmation of this interesting hypothesis.

We remain perplexed, therefore, and can only look

with wonder upon these images of ancient London. The first of them depicts a group of people gathered beside the Thames; they seem to be engaged in some tribal rite, during which they clap their hands and smile at one another. Perhaps they intend to worship the river, or to offer a sacrifice to the city, since the next scenes are those of a naked woman, with a band of striped linen around her neck, floating upon the water. It is possible that this body was part of an elaborate ceremony designed to summon up the dead from the depths of the river, but the very texture of Mouldwarp life is too rapid and discontinuous to allow any certain judgement.

The next representations, for example, are taken within some interior space where a male human is wrapping the same band of striped linen around his own neck. Is he one of the dead who has been reborn? Or is he about to become a willing sacrifice? There are no others in his presence, which suggests that he has been exiled from the city. Then he walks down to the ground by means of wooden steps or stairs and somehow reappears in a room filled with glass bottles. The nature of Mouldwarp life is disconcerting indeed, with sudden leaps of time and space which do not seem to affect the inhabitants of this continually evolving world. The exile pours liquid into a glass and swallows it in one gesture. This may be a form of awakening. He then places a tube of paper or cloth into his mouth and lights it; here we notice the worship of fire as well as water. He must be the only inhabitant of this bottle-chamber, since his name is inscribed upon a frosted glass exterior; he is called Nell Gwyn. Immediately opposite him dwells Henrietta Street, who cannot be seen.

Once again, in one of those extraordinary transitions of ancient city life, Nell Gwyn has suddenly passed through a doorway into the thoroughfare beyond. Here, then, was our first sight of the primitive city. It has been a constant source of excitement and surprise to us, sometimes overwhelming to those observing it for the first time. We glimpse doors and stairways, which seem to lead into unseen interior spaces, and we are almost afraid that we will fall into the depths of the strange world! The narrow path itself is filled with human figures engaged in harmonious movement, as if being directed by some unseen power; there are many objects piled high behind glass windows, and in certain places people give notes or coins in exchange for these objects. Then, in a moment, all this has been transformed into a great courtyard where wooden containers are piled with variously coloured fruits. The name of 'Covent Garden' can be seen—it is likely that there were many such gardens throughout the old city. In the next image Nell Gwyn is being given a selection of green and orange fruits by a red-headed priest or servant, while behind them are posters encouraging the citizens to further efforts— 'Courage' can be seen as Nell Gwyn leaves the garden.

No history of Mouldwarp had mentioned this, which serves to emphasise that our knowledge of the past is conjectural at best. By careful interpretation of these images, however, we have devised a model of ancient London in which every four thoroughfares meet in a garden, where food was freely distributed. From the evidence of Hitchcock Frenzy we have also concluded that each object in the Mouldwarp world was painted, and that the citizens coloured their own bodies. It is worth remarking that the paths and thoroughfares of London differ in size and length. The fact that some are wide and others narrow seems to have determined the nature of the people who inhabited them as well as the events which occurred there.

Nell Gwyn has once more moved instantaneously to quite another dwelling. It has the characteristic frosted window with the name of the owner, Pig and Whistle, inscribed upon it. Pig and Whistle's friends can be seen drinking from glass vessels and, like Nell Gwyn, they place lighted paper in their mouths; it is probable that this form of fire worship also provided food and energy to its devotees. Two citizens enter, taking coverings from their heads; perhaps the external air is harmful to them, or they need to be protected from its weight. Nell Gwyn has put a large piece of paper before his face, as if he were trying to conceal himself; yet perhaps the paper is speaking to him, since numbers appear before us: 4.30, 20–1. In this mathematical world, perhaps they conversed only in figures! Nell Gwyn salutes Pig and Whistle, and is seen walking down a stone thoroughfare. The grey birds cluster around him, but he alarms them with a sudden movement; it has been suggested that these fly- ing creatures are the ancestors of our angels, subdued and darkened by the conditions of Mouldwarp, but at best this is conjecture. Suddenly it is night. We know this because the sky has gone, the colours have faded, and small lights have appeared in various dwellings. Hitchcock Frenzy also now fades into darkness, since the strip of images is broken at this point.

29

Plato: May I ask a favour of you?

Soul: Whatever I have is yours.

Plato: Tell me about the people of Mouldwarp. Were they as deluded as we are taught? As I teach?

Soul: Who can say? I would never presume to contradict you, of course, but there may have been occasions when they wondered what was happening to them. There may even have been moments when they did not know what they were supposed to be doing. I can recall—oh, nothing.

Plato: What were you about to say? You were going to be indiscreet. You were on the point of telling me that you were acquainted with them at first hand. I knew it. You were there.

Soul: Please don't put words into my—

Plato: You misled me.

Soul: This interview is now ended.

Plato: No. Don't go. I apologise.

Soul: Promise?

Plato: Promise.

Soul: We will pretend we never spoke of such matters. You were asking me about Mouldwarp, I believe?

Plato: Yes. What if I was wrong or mistaken about the people of that time?

Soul: Sometimes, you know, I worry about you.

Plato: Why?

Soul: You have no perspective.

Plato: But surely that is your responsibility?

Soul: Let me put it this way. What if you were meant to be wrong? What if that was the only way to maintain confidence in the reality of the present world?

Plato: It would be a very hard destiny.

Soul: It might also be an inevitable one. If every age depends upon wilful blindness, then you, Plato, become necessary.

Plato: So is that your purpose? To preserve my ignorance?

Soul: I have no purpose. I am simply here.

Plato: I do not believe you.

Soul: What are you saying? You do not believe your own soul? That is impossible.

Plato: I am confused. I admit it. Help me.

Soul: I will make an agreement with you. You need to reach the limits of your knowledge and your belief. Am I correct?

Plato: Of course.

Soul: Then I will no longer protect you.

Plato: Protect me against what?

Soul: I don't know. It is normally the duty of the soul to defend her charge—

Plato: I once saw the picture of an angel with a flaming sword.

Soul: That sort of thing. But if you really wish to discover some truth—

Plato: That is my desire.

Soul: Then so be it. I will no longer stand in its way. Good luck.

Plato: When will I see you again?

Soul: Have you ever really seen me? Go now. The citizens are waiting for you.

30

You see the charred paper before you? Please note that it contains words in an early English script. I have employed square brackets in order to signify a tentative conjectural meaning, and asterisks to denote a tear or burn in the manuscript itself. It reads as follows, and you will forgive me if my accent sounds harsh or discordant. It is considered to be authentic.

> fragments [they] have * ruins
> *ieronymo * * again
>
> > > * * Eliot

It is my contention that 'Eliot' here signifies the name of the author or singer of the quoted lines and, fortunately, there is surviving evidence which may lead us to a closer identification. A fragment of prose has been recovered which alludes to 'the writer George Eliot', and in a collection of Mouldwarp frescos which can provisionally be dated somewhere between the eighteenth and twenty-first centuries there exists a wall painting or wall chart with the inscription 'The Alhambra. Presenting Our Very Own Eliot, the Chocolate-Coloured Crooner and Nimble Negro'. I have already informed you that in this epoch the earth was divided and dispersed into 'races', generally considered to have arisen for climatic rather than spiritual reasons; 'negro' or 'chocolate-coloured', then, are variants of 'African' or 'black'. In the succeeding Age of Witspell, of course, it was believed that the black 'races' were closer to God and had therefore been burned by the rays of divine love. It can be suggested, therefore, that these lines are the work of an African singer named George Eliot. In this there can be no certainty, as I am only too well aware, but the identification has at least the merit of being supported by all the available evidence.

The text itself has been subject to various interpretations. One historian asserts that

$$\text{fragments} = \text{ruins}$$

and that George Eliot is simply contemplating the remains of some chapel or shrine of an earlier age built in

homage to 'ieronymo' or St Jerome. But that suggestion
has been challenged by another reader, who infers that

ruins = runes

and that 'ieronymo' can then be reworked as

i.e. my roon

or 'that is my spell'. I, Plato, have developed this
point with the inference that the black singer was in
fact prophesying the fall of the Age of Mouldwarp into
ruins and fragments. If I may quote my own words
on that occasion, 'Consider the plight of the poets or
singers of that epoch who (as we believe) had the role
only of entertainers. It is not clear whether they gave
recitations in public places or at private gatherings, but
their lowly status is confirmed by the paucity of material relating to them and the characteristically melan-
choly tone of their surviving works.' It has even been
surmised that George Eliot deliberately created a 'fragment' or 'ruin' of a poem in order to exemplify his despair. There may indeed have been a long tradition of
ruin literature of which he was perhaps the last expo-
nent. Excuse me. My light is beginning to fade. You
had noticed it already? Please, there is no need for
alarm. There is no sickness. Nothing will harm you. I
am tired. That is all. This oration is completed.

31

Something is happening. Something is coming. I can hear cries and murmuring voices, and now the shadows have started to appear. I feel their presence all around me. Soul! I have certain anxieties. I feel them more strongly than you can possibly imagine. Soul? Where are you? Now I can see a pale young man leaning against a post. There is a girl. There is an animal approaching her. The name becoming visible is

Golden Lane. Who are these people walking beside me? There are so many. And they are much closer than I ever knew. Now there is the rushing of a great wind. Soul! Is this why you once guarded me? Were you protecting me against them?

32

Sidonia: So you saw him?

Ornatus: He was standing just outside the crippled gate.

Sidonia: Curious. That is not his customary spot.

Ornatus: And there was another peculiar thing: he was talking to himself.

Sidonia: No!

Ornatus: I could see him gesticulating, too. He looked very fierce.

Sidonia: Could you hear anything he said?

Ornatus: Something about a golden lane. And the crowds all about him. Yet there was no one there except himself. Then he came up to me.

Sidonia: What did you do?

Ornatus: I offered him reverence and he bowed in return. We should have remained silent, according to custom—

Sidonia: Of course.

Ornatus: But he suddenly asked me if I was waiting for someone.

Sidonia: What?

Ornatus: 'I am not waiting,' I said, 'I am simply being still. It is holy to be still.' Then he laughed.

Sidonia: And so you laughed?

Ornatus: Naturally. Then he asked me if I was thinking about anything. 'Nothing at all,' I replied. He asked me why not. 'It is not compulsory to think,' I told him; 'it is not like dreaming.'

Sidonia: Well put.

Ornatus: Thank you. Then he put his hand across his face and mentioned that he had seen me in the race against the oarsmen of Essex Street. He asked me if I had won—

Sidonia: What an extraordinary question.

Ornatus: And I had to explain to him, just as if he were a child, that no one was expected to win. He laughed again. Then he asked me if that was why I looked so sad.

Sidonia: Can he be losing his mind?

Ornatus: He did say something about losing his soul, but it was so ridiculous that I pretended not to listen. Then, after a moment, he mentioned that he was going on a journey.

Sidonia: A journey? You mean—

Ornatus: When you leave the city.

Sidonia: Whatever for?

Ornatus: That is precisely what I asked him.

Sidonia: And what did he say?

Ornatus: He looked around and murmured something about other places. Other people. I said, 'Listen to me, Plato.' That is how I addressed him.

Sidonia: Not as an orator?

Ornatus: No. That seemed somehow unimportant. Or unnecessary. 'Listen to me, Plato. We have all grown up together within the city. We have obeyed its injunctions. We have been instructed in its mysteries. You yourself were chosen to guide us with your oratory. We spend our lives contemplating its goodness and beauty. We hear you expounding upon its inner harmonies. Why try and discover something else beyond its Wall?' He gave a curious answer.

Sidonia: Which was?

Ornatus: 'Perhaps, dear Ornatus, I am not travelling as far as you think. Perhaps it is possible to embark upon a journey while remaining in the same place.'

Sidonia: What did he mean by that?

Ornatus: I have absolutely no idea. Come. Shall we take a skiff down the Fleet and search for angels' feathers?

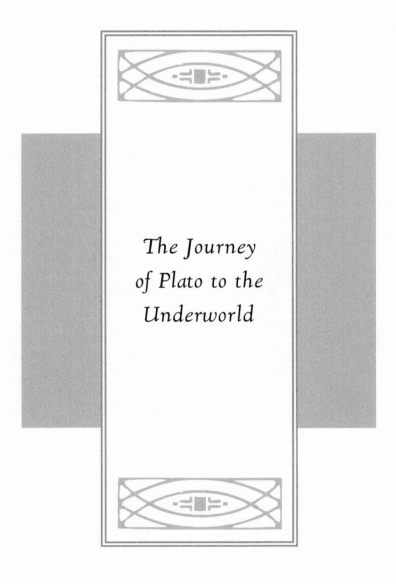

*The Journey
of Plato to the
Underworld*

33

There was a cave, and the ground sloped downwards. I sensed the smell of that which was neither living nor dead. I believed that I could hear voices and I began walking towards the mouth of the cave. I admit to a slight sense of fear, but I submit that all of us share some horror of darkness. You tell me that I was dreaming? This was no dream. I was as wakeful and as watchful as I have ever been.

When I entered the cave the air seemed so heavy that, for a moment, I believed I could go no further.

But the ground still sloped downwards and instinc-
tively I bowed my head as I walked into the darkness.
I do not know how far I travelled. It is possible that I
did not move at all. Perhaps I stood still. Surely you
understand? It had grown to such a pitch of blackness
that I could not see my own body, or feel aware of any
movement. I realised later, of course, what had happened. I was changing dimensions in order to enter the
world of Mouldwarp. Who cried out that 'Plato is impious'? I am not impious! I am simply telling you the
truth. The darkness began to lift, very slowly, and I
noticed that a sombre radiance seemed to emanate from
the stone around me. It was the colour of fire or blood.
I was still walking down. Forgive me. I can only express it as 'up' and 'down'. Perhaps I have become
like them.

I knew, somehow, that I was following a circular
path. It was growing warmer and I noticed that in the
glowing light my body cast a strange shape upon the
ground. It was called a shadow, or a wraith created by
the false light of their sun. Theirs was a world of shadows. Then I found myself before a flight of broad stone
stairs. I had no choice. I stepped upon the first stair.
I began to descend, but once more it was as if I were
not moving at all; I might have remained in the same
place, except that various layers of dark and light
passed over my head. I experienced the strangest sensations of stupor, and of anxious restlessness, until I
recognised that I was experiencing night and day as

they once were in antiquity. The intervals between them grew longer, until I was able to glimpse points of light in the darkness. I looked up. I looked up and saw the bright objects once called stars. There was a firmament stretching above me, and the position of the night sky was very like that which I had studied in the old charts of Mouldwarp. These were the ancient fixed stars, shining below the level of our world!

Then the noise began. At first it was the merest whispering, but it grew steadily louder until it filled my ears with chiming, and tapping, and rhythmic thudding. There were more violent indistinct sounds, but the path had become so steep that there was no chance of turning back. But why should I wish to return, when I could run towards my vision? I had come into a great cavern extending in every direction. It was impossible to gauge its depth, or its height, although I could see the fixed stars still turning overhead. And there, stretching below me, was London! It was no longer night but broad day and I could see great towers of glass, domes, roofs and houses. I saw the Thames itself, gleaming in the distance, with wide thoroughfares running beside it. The avenues and buildings were more elaborate and extensive than anything we had ever surmised; yet, somehow, this was the city of which I had always dreamed.

How can I describe to you all the strangeness of my journey among the people of Mouldwarp? They were short, little more than half your height, and even I had to walk carefully among them. You ask if they were alarmed by my appearance, but the truth is that they could not see me. It was as if I were a ghost or spirit. Why do you laugh? I believe that I was not visible to them because I still existed in dimensions other than their own. That is why they were so compact, so densely formed, and why all their activity was curiously restrained. They moved in preordained patterns—sometimes it seemed that they did not know in which direction they were travelling. Their eyes were focused ahead and yet they seemed to see nothing; they might have been wrapped in intense thought, but of what were they thinking?

I bent over to listen to them; I tried to speak, but of course they could not hear me. I travelled down Old Street and saw that it was once a track in the wilderness. I came into Smithfield and flinched at the anger of those who lived beside it. In Cheapside the city itself had established intricate patterns of movement, and all the activity of the citizens was for its own sake. In Clapham I listened to them talking—*have you got the time please he obviously wants the best price but he wants to sell as well I shall be off then shall I he never wants to hear the truth can you possibly tell me the time.* And so their lives continued. They had no way of knowing that their earth was in a great cavern beneath the surface of our world. Their sky was the roof of a cave, but for them it was the threshold of the universe. I was walking among the blind. Yet when at night I looked up at the glittering face of the Mouldwarp heaven I, too, was entranced by it.

I had thought that, when each night followed day, there would be silence and stillness; instead there was continual sound. When I walked in any direction, trying to find its source, it retreated from me with every step. It was then I heard it; this was the whispering and groaning of London itself. Neither was there any true darkness, since the horizons of the city glowed beneath the darker levels of the air. Beside the streets there were vessels of glass, or frozen water, which contained the radiance of the stars. Could I have invented such a place? The citizens wore close-fitting garments of many colours. I had expected them to be uniform in appearance, but instead they seemed to mock and parody each other. They seemed to delight in difference and to believe that there was no distinction between outward and inward. Does this surprise you? Only then did I begin to understand the nature of the Mouldwarp era. Of course they could not escape the tyranny of their dimensions, or the restrictions of their life within the cave, but this afforded them extra delight in contrast and discontinuity. Within the precincts of government and of business, of living and of working, they derived great pleasure from reversals and oppositions. The air was tainted by the inhuman smell of numbers and machines, but the city itself was in a state of perpetual change. No. Do not laugh. Listen to me. I soon discovered that they always wished to communicate in the shortest possible time; the most simple piece of information seemed to amuse them, as long as it could be gathered instantaneously. There was one other aspect of their lives which, I admit, I ought to have anticipated: the faster an action could be reported, the more significance it acquired. Events themselves were not of any consequence, only the fact that they could be known quickly. Now you are silent. Again I ask you: how could I have invented such a reality?

When the citizens were young they tried to leap into the air; when they were old they stooped downwards to the earth, which they believed to be their final home. They did not know that they lived in confinement, and many were content. Perhaps they were happy simply because they fulfilled their form, but I also saw those who were tired and careworn. They were continually building and rebuilding their city. They took pleasure in destruction, I believe, because it allowed them a kind of forgetfulness. So the city continued to spread, encroaching upon new ground. It was continually going forward, forever seeking some harmonious outline without ever finding it. I tell you this: Mouldwarp London had no boundaries. It had no beginning and no end. That is why its citizens also seemed so restless. They were consumed by the need for activity, but it was activity for its own sake. There may be a further explanation. It is possible that they continued at their fevered pace in the belief that if the pattern was interrupted they, as well as the city itself, might be destroyed. So there was a time for eating, a time for sleeping, a time for working. There was even a band of time strapped to their wrists, like a manacle binding them to life in the cave. They lived in small divisions or fragments of time, continually anticipating the conclusion of each fragment as if the whole point of activity lay in its end.

Their time was everywhere. It forced them to go forward. When I saw them walking in great lines, it was time itself that was moving. But it was not uniform. I had expected it to be forever racing, never ceasing, but in fact it proceeded at different speeds according to the variable nature of the city. There were certain areas where it moved quickly, and others where it went forward reluctantly or fitfully— and there were places where it no longer moved at all. There were narrow streets in the city where I could still hear the voices of those who had passed through many years before. Then I made another wonderful discovery. There were some citizens of Mouldwarp who seemed to live in a different time. There were ragged people who wandered with dogs; they were not on the same journey as those whom they passed on the crowded thoroughfares. There were children who chanted songs from an earlier age and there were old people who already had the look of eternity upon their faces. You laugh at me. But I, Plato, have seen and heard these things. May I continue? They could sometimes glimpse images or ghosts of the spirit, but they would look away in disbelief or consternation. On occasions I noticed that one of them would intercept a brief look from some unknown citizen—both would glance at each other, and pass on, as if nothing mysterious had occurred. I knew then that their souls were trying to communicate, even through the fog and darkness of Mouldwarp. The ancient forms of speech and prayer were still in existence, but barely able to stir beneath the burden of this reality. So I heard words which the citizens could not hear, and observed moments of recognition or glances of longing which they never saw.

But their souls felt my presence, and some of them rose up in their cells to greet me. I welcomed them in turn and began to converse with them. We were not heard, of course, by those whom we sought to understand. I first asked these tiny chattering spirits about their own beliefs, but they possessed none— or otherwise they were so confused and uncertain that it would have been better if they had had none. They were ashamed of their own uncertainty but, as they told me, they had been held in the dark so long that they scarcely recognised one another.

I tried to learn more about the history of this city, but no one seemed to know it. They had heard of giants in the past, the original inhabitants of London—

'Now we believe,' they said, 'that they were prophe-
cies of you and your race'! I had so many questions.
Did these trees collect the shadows of the people who
passed beneath? They had no answer. They did not
even know the names of the trees. I asked them if the
areas of grass were sacred places. I asked them why the
buildings aspired to the sky. The birds that clustered
on the roofs and in the squares—were they the guardians of London? Do sundials control the sun? They did
not understand my questions. Instead they complained
to me that they were imprisoned within beings who
had little concept of divinity or truth, but who instead
worshipped order and control. They told me that the
people of Mouldwarp professed to care for their world,
but they killed their unborn children and treated their
animal companions with great savagery. Yet still they
wanted to make copies of themselves by means of their
science. I am telling you these things without wishing
to disturb you. I intend to hide nothing of the truth
from you, revealing both good and evil so that you can
decide for yourselves whether I have visited a real city.

I conversed once more with these little spirits, and
they told me that their charges suffered from forgetfulness and fear. The citizens were often bewildered;
they lived within fantasies and ambitions which the
city itself had created, and they felt obliged to act according to the roles allotted to them. They had no understanding of themselves. They had no use for the
present except as an avenue to the future, and yet

many experienced a great horror of death. They desired to go faster and faster, but towards some unknown destination. No wonder their souls shivered in the darkness. I spoke to some who simply wished to be dissolved and to disappear. When I heard people arguing, I saw their perturbed spirits fluttering above them.

I remember walking by the sacred Thames, where the outcasts slept, when a young man passed by me sighing. His soul recognised my presence and she spoke to me softly. 'Do you see this river? I have stared into its depths and I have come to the conclusion that it is never the same. It exists for a moment, but then it is changed by water from other rivers and other seas. How can this be so? How can it always be the same and always different? Ever fresh and ever renewed?' I had no answer but, after they had gone, I gazed upon its surface. And there for the first time in this world I saw the outline of my own face, rippling upon the water. I saw myself ebbing and flowing in time. I looked up and gazed at their sun; the disc shone hot and bright, but I could see through it to the other side and to the roof of the cave. It was then I decided to return and to tell you of my discoveries.

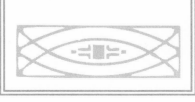

*The Trial of
Plato Charged
with Corrupting
the Young by
Spinning Lies
and Fables*

34

Sparkler: And then what did he do?

Ornatus: He was standing beside the river, with a crowd gathered around him. You should have seen him, stamping his foot and dancing and singing out his words. He has the voice of a tall man—

Sparkler: He always possessed gifts beyond his stature. That is why his light is so intense.

Ornatus: He cannot help his nature, of course, but he makes a point of mentioning it. He revels in it. 'Consider my plight,' he says. 'I am different from all of you. Even the children look down on me.' Then he pauses for a moment. 'But I wonder who looks down on you?'

Sparkler: What did he mean by that?

Ornatus: Only he knows. Nothing, probably. But he captured their attention. That was when he began talking about science. Or was it silence? Apparently silence created food and clothes and everything else.

Sparkler: Where has he found this? It cannot have been taught to him, since the guardians would never sanction such nonsense.

Ornatus: That is what I have been trying to tell you. You never listen.

Sparkler: And you are too impatient.

Ornatus: He found it all in a cave.

Sparkler: A cave? What kind of cave?

Ornatus: I have to admit I missed most of it. I was anointing my feet.

Sparkler: As usual.

Ornatus: But then he mentioned clocks. Or locks. The locks signified time. It was all very confusing. Let me see if I can reawaken the scene.

Do you see this? Come closer, citizens. It is known as a watch. I brought it back with me from the cave of Mouldwarp. No. Do not laugh. Listen. These marks are called numbers. Notice how this narrow strip of metal sweeps around in a circle of harmony? That is time. Do not be afraid to touch it. Its spell cannot be

122

reawakened. What was its purpose? It created a universe! Examine the numbers around the rim. Do they not make beautiful shapes? See the curvature of this one. Look at the oval. They are wonderful because they once represented the structure of the world. If we open the back, here, we find tiny springs and wheels. This is the machine. There was once a whole universe modelled in its shape. That is why this watch was once an object of great power. The people of Mouldwarp believed that they were the inhabitants of time and that time itself was sacred because it was involved in the origin of all things. Do you begin to understand what an interesting civilisation it was? Time lent them a sense of progress and of change, as well as giving them perspective and an indication of distance. It allowed them hope and also forgetfulness. There was a thing called art, which was also the production of time. Other great achievements were performed in its name and the ancient citizens, who lived in so few dimensions, were astonished by it. So they created this ritual object, this watch.

But then Plato made an extraordinary announcement.
Sparkler: About what?
Ornatus: He claimed that his orations had been filled with errors and misinterpretations.
Sparkler: No!
Ornatus: Mouldwarp had not ended in chaos. There had been no burning of the machines.

Sparkler: This is absurd! What did the citizens make of it?

Ornatus: Some of them were bewildered. Some were laughing. I just walked away. I was strolling in the fields among the archers when I heard the rumour that he has been put on trial.

Sparkler: Precisely what I have heard. We shared a parish and a school with him, but we did not foresee any of this.

35

We have listened to you carefully, Plato. We have considered everything you have told us. We cannot judge you on your conscience, only upon what you have said and done. It is our duty now to repeat the charges against you, so that you may answer them directly.

If you can convince me with argument, then of course I will retract.

The first charge against you is that you have corrupted the youth of this city by your words and speeches.

How can there be corruption in teaching them to

consider the world not as it is but as it might have been? Or as it once was?

Already you are contradicting yourself. In your statement of exculpation to us, you have insisted that this world still exists in some dark cavern beneath our city. You have described it in such vivid detail that some of us long to visit.

(Laughter)

Yes. We do exist above them. We are, to them, no more than ghosts of light—

You were in a drunken stupor and dreamed all of this.

May I be allowed to continue? Their city is sunk within a cave and their sky is the roof of that dark chamber. I will debate with you on the merits of two realities existing simultaneously, and together we may decide that all versions and visions of the world may coexist eternally. But I have taught the young nothing of this. Shall I tell you what I said to them?

36

Help me forward, children. If I stand upon the top of
the hill, I can be seen by you all. There once stood a
great domed church on this summit, dedicated to the
god Paul. I have seen it. There was a churchyard here.
I am pleased that it is now a desert place. Do you
know why? It means that I can speak freely to you
without the whispers and rumours of the citizens. I am
Plato the witless. That is what they call me now. Perhaps there is some justice there. I have always taught
that you must know yourself. That is why I have

looked into myself, too, and I realise I am not always right. I make mistakes. I stumble towards the truth. Look. Here is one of the stones I stumbled upon. It is not a witless stone like me, however. It is not one of the stones scattered around us. It is a witty stone. Do you see the marks carved upon its sides? Stones such as this were known to the ancients as dice. I brought it back with me from—you know where. Shall we follow the pattern of our ancestors? Roll the stone. Now roll it again. Can any of you tell me why different sides appeared? Can anyone predict which side will be hidden on the third roll? Of course you cannot. That is why I stumble. That is why I stop and think. Let us suppose that after a hundred, or even a thousand, throws we could still not be sure which side it would turn upon. Can we doubt that the anxiety would begin to affect our own lives? Why do we speak of human certainty, when this little stone will always trip us up? Perhaps I am being witless again. Perhaps not.

Of course it may be that our ancestors were not so frightened of change, and of chance, as we are. Perhaps it became, for them, a game like this one. I believe that they were content to face all the troubles and misadventures of this world. I have taught you that they lived in darkness, but they were not always afraid of the dark. I have already explained to you how they saw burning objects in their sky, which brought them warmth and comfort, but what if they had been granted other gifts? There is no darkness upon this little stone. It is a light and pleasant thing. Feel it. It reminds us that wherever there is fear, there is also delight; where there is pain, there may also be pleasure.

That is why I love those among you who are willing to question. I know that you have been taught the lives of gods and of heroes, of angels and of giants. But you have never heard the legends of those who stood alone against the world and, by dint of courage and truthfulness, won their battles. Why not praise them as well as the leaders who have been chosen for you to study? Look how different you all are. The son of Artemidorus is taller and more fair-skinned than the son of Madrigal; the daughter of Ornatus has limbs more slender than the daughter of Magnolia. Let us suppose that you are all different in other ways. I do not doubt that you will then approach the moment of revelation which once came to me. That is when I cried out, 'I am I! I am not someone other!' There. I have shouted it out, once more, and the city walls have not crumbled. Let us go down now and pray together by the black friars.

37

Was there any harm, or danger, in my words to them? On our way down from the hill I asked them to consider the nature of our gestures—how we stand back in conversation and raise our hands, how we touch our faces to denote pity or pleasure, how we close our eyes to signify assent. These are not newly made. They reach back for many thousands of years.

Enough! You are on trial for spreading fables and deceits, Plato. You are not invited to elaborate upon them.

I will make one confession to you. I seemed to recollect something of myself in the citizens of Mould-warp. In many ways they were as barbarous and foolish as I have described; but when I looked into their eyes, or whispered to their souls, I recognised that they were indeed our ancestors. That is perhaps why I loved them. They could not know that they lived in a cave, hidden from the light. But how can we be sure that, in turn, there is not a world of brightness beyond our own?

Once more you test our patience, Plato. Do not cling to your blasphemies.

I see that I have offended you. You condemn me because I cannot accept the ultimate reality of our world. Is that it?

You know very well the case against you. You have departed from the way. You will attract misfortune. The citizens already murmur against you.

How can it be that I disturb them by speaking the truth and admitting that in my orations I have misled them?

You are being too modest. You have gone further than that.

How? I have never spoken evil of the angels. I have never questioned the sanctity of mazes and mirrors. I have never defied the hierarchy of colours. I have beaten the bounds of my parish, according to custom. Do you want me to go on?

This is mere sophistry, Plato. All of us know that by your words you have divided children from their parents. Do you wish us to give you an example?

38

Ornatus: Come closer, Myander. Sit by me. I see that you have been crying.

Myander: You know why, father. I have been told that I must move to another part of the city.

Ornatus: All children of a certain age move on. It is the custom. It gives you further cause to worship and to understand.

Myander: But why is it necessary to move at all? I have seen citizens, in the market and in the streets, who have stood in one place always.

Ornatus: They suffer from sickness. They are to be pitied, not condemned. They believe that our dimensions are illusory and so they refuse to make even the smallest movement.

Myander: Plato says that we resemble them because we rarely walk beyond the walls.

Ornatus: Plato says many things, Myander. Not all of them are right. We do not move beyond the city because there is no reason to do so. This is our companionship. The light around us is the light of human care. It is life itself. Why wander beyond our bounds, where we could only grow weary?

Myander: Yet Plato—

Ornatus: Oh. Once more.

Myander: Plato says that we must learn to doubt and to question all these things. I was listening to him by the bishop's gate.

When I was a child, as you are, I was taken to see the lambs on the green of Lambeth. 'Look, Plato,' my instructor said to me, 'look how they frisk and gambol.' 'Why?' I asked. 'Because that is what lambs have always done. They know they have been chosen to fulfil their form, and they rejoice. And that is what you must do, little Plato.' Did I agree or disagree? What do you think? I am short, like you. I admit it. How can I deny it, when I have to stand back and look up at the citizens? You can laugh, if you wish. I do, often. It fills me with joy to know that I am different. When I was a

133

child my mother told me never to accept the opinions of others without examining them carefully. 'You are small,' she said to me, 'because you have been chosen to see everything from a different vantage.' So I learned to study myself rather than study the lessons that others wished to teach me. I wanted to find the truth that was true for me alone. Do you understand me? Here is an ancient coin. If you come close, you will see it.

Then he put it in his left palm and moved his hands one over the other.

Is it still there, where I placed it? Of course? No. It has gone. It is in my right hand. And children are supposed to be so observant! This is my only suggestion to you. There are no certainties. So take nothing for granted. Question your instructors. Ask them this: 'How can I be sure what existence I have been chosen for?'

Ornatus: So that is how he speaks to you.
Myander: He does not treat us as children. He argues with us.

Why is sleep supposed to be a holy thing? Because it is a form of worship. But then why do I sleep only fitfully?

And then he contradicts us.

To wait, and to do nothing, is a form of worship. Is that what you were taught? But what if worship were a form of waiting? Waiting for what?

Sometimes he even mocks us.

So you have heard of the city of the unborn. But you do not know where it is. It is the city from which we all have come, but its location does not interest you. It might disturb the deep peace of your being. Is that the phrase? Yes? The deep peace of being. But I tell you this. In the house of birth, just outside the walls, the newborn scream and struggle as they are brought into our world. Tell me, why is this?

Ornatus: There is no need to listen to him, Myander. Even better, try to avoid him. I have been told something. I have learned that he is placed on trial.
Myander: So much the worse for us.

39

Do you understand now how you have disturbed the citizens?

Never once have I described my journey to the children. I have simply invited them to ask questions and
to discuss the answers among themselves.

*You mention your famous journey once again. May we
then be permitted to ask our own questions? What if you had
stood before the citizens of Mouldwarp and informed them
that they were living in a dark and shrunken world? That
they were imprisoned within a cave. Do you think they would
have applauded you and offered you thanks? Do you imagine*

that they would have been grateful for this knowledge? No.
They would have scorned you as a simpleton, or condemned
you as a deluder.

As you do.

We do not consider you to be foolish and we have not yet
condemned you. If it is a matter of delusion, perhaps it is only
self-delusion.

You mean that I have lost my wits. Thank you.

No. You protest too much. In certain respects we sympa-
thise with you.

I do not require sympathy. I do not believe that I
need it. I only ask to be judged with fairness. It has
been suggested that I invented my journey to Mouldwarp in order to gain credit for myself. What credit?
I now stand before you as a man about to be condemned. It was put to me that all was fantasy, designed
to prove my own speculations about our ancestors.
Could anyone have invented the world I have described?

To imagine a world within our world—a world beneath
our world. It is impossible.

Yet I have explained to you my horror within the
cave and I have admitted my confusion. I had expected
them to worship the stars they had created, but they
scarcely noticed them. I had expected them to be afraid
of the dark that time had formed, but instead they
filled it with lights. I had believed them to be cele-
brants of power, but they simply chattered to one another, hour by hour, about nothing in particular. How
could I possibly have dreamed of this? When I spoke

to their souls, the unhappy voices were a revelation; they asked me questions, but I dared not answer in case I spread terror among them. Why should I invent such things, only to be greeted with laughter by you all? I tell you, I have seen a real world.

You say that they were constrained by this—time— which did not even exist. So they were enslaved to a concept which they themselves had invented? Do you expect us to believe this?

I—

You say that they did not worship their stars. So what god did they reverence?

It is not a question of—

They had no god. The people of Mouldwarp believed that they lived in a material world. Is that so?

It is so.

Knowing that material is finite, then, they decided to conquer rather than to worship time and the stars. They proclaimed their liberty, and yet they were slaves of instinct and suggestion. They declared their freedom of speech and freedom of belief, and yet they were never really free. All this we deduce from your own account.

You speak of slavish instinct, but I saw energy and exhilaration. Perhaps you are correct in believing that they wished to conquer their material world, but this afforded them a sense of progress.

But why, then, did they have no sense of the sacred?

They did not need it! They were truly free, since they believed that they were in control of their own destinies. Think of your own lives now. They are empty, precisely because you wish them to be without meaning. You believe that there is no meaning.

That is false. We know that we are the meaning. This session is now ended. Let the bells ring out.

40

Madrigal: Did you attend the session?

Sidonia: Of course. It was entertaining. Plato and the guardians stood opposite each other on the hills, while we sat between them on the banks of the Fleet.

Madrigal: Ornatus told me that he could hear the voices of the guardians from the bridge. They sounded, to him, very vibrant. Very expressive. He could also hear the citizens murmuring.

Sidonia: Some of them were tired. I had brought my own resting place, because I knew that it was going to be a long affair. As one citizen said, we might have entered another new age before it was finished. Even Plato laughed at that.

Madrigal: But surely Plato is talking nonsense? There is no above or below. No outward or inward. Nothing that exists is hidden from human sight.

Sidonia: Apparently not. But Plato has always defied our expectations.

Madrigal: And how could he have ventured into this underground world of Mouldwarp if it only existed in three or four dimensions?

Sidonia: He would certainly feel the pinch. Why are you laughing?

Madrigal: Did you hear the funny story from Sparkler?

Sidonia: What story?

Madrigal: He was going towards the temple to be healed, when Plato stopped him. Do you know what he said? 'Better that you should explore your illness and learn from your suffering, Sparkler, rather than desire to be cured.'

Sidonia: I suppose Sparkler had something to say about that?

Madrigal: Oh yes. 'Plato,' he said, 'you may think you are a very clever person. You have always been clever, ever since we first met at the ceremony of naming. But sometimes, I believe, you know nothing.'

Sidonia: And Plato?

Madrigal: He danced.

Sidonia: What?

Madrigal: He danced upon the earth. And then he replied with some kind of chant. 'Sparkler,' he sang, 'your light still sparkles but you do not see. I am clever *because* I know nothing.'

Sidonia: What an extraordinary statement! And yet, in Plato's case, I have become accustomed to the extraordinary.

4I

Sidonia: I am concerned for you. You seem lost to us.

Plato: Does it matter?

Sidonia: But in your arguments you miss so much. Our world is gentler than you admit. Do you know, for example, what I do when I am alone? I float in a dream of my own and, sometimes, the angels join me.

Plato: Do you speak to them?

Sidonia: No. They whisper to me, but I can never understand them.

Plato: They have been with us since the beginning of the world and still they can only whisper.

Sidonia: Sometimes I hear them in music.

Plato: And in the voices of children.

Sidonia: But why are they here?

Plato: There is no other place for them. Yet at the same time they exist everywhere. This is what I am now beginning to understand—

Sidonia: I was conversing with Madrigal—

Plato: Madrigal is very wise, but he is impatient for the truth. He does not listen. Sparkler and Ornatus are the same. Yet that is not so strange. The parishioners of Newgate are known for their bad temper, and those of St Giles for their charity. So in turn the citizens of our parish may be known for their impatience.

Sidonia: The impatient inhabitants of Pie Corner? An interesting theory. That was what I was telling Madrigal. From you, Plato, he must expect the unusual.

Plato: There sounds the bell for the next session. I hope that I can satisfy him.

42

Throw yourself upon our mercy, Plato. Trust us.

I can trust only my destiny. Whether I stand or fall here, I could not have acted otherwise. I can no more change my life than I can alter the colour of my eyes. They are white, like yours, and my conscience is white.

Conscience is knowledge with others. Here we are all one city. We are the limbs of the city. We are a common body. How can you wish to part yourself from us?

I have been granted a vision and I must declare it. I can do no other.

You know well enough that we can have no separate visions. It is impossible. Worse: it is blasphemy.

I do not act alone, as you seem to think. I have my soul. She led me forward on my journey.

43

Plato: Where were you when I needed you, in Golden Lane?

Soul: You always need me. And, you must admit, I ask for very little in return. But I will ask you this: are you determined to go forward into the cave?

Plato: Forward? It may be backward.

Soul: You were the one who wished to visit this place. I am here to accompany you, not to lead you.

Plato: The rain might fall here, as it did in the old days. The wind might blow and the dew form.

Soul: The old days. Always the old days. Can you survive the heat of their false sun? Can you live in their dust?

Plato: I admit that I am afraid of those things. I am afraid of their teeming life. Of their blind instinct to grow. Listen. Can you hear the voices?

Soul: I hear nothing.

Plato: I feel that I am close to them.

Soul: You may have heard them. But are you sure that they are not within your own mind?

44

More blasphemy. Our souls do not speak to us.

How can you be sure?

Our souls do not appear to us.

That is not true. I slept after my journey and, when
I awoke, she was sitting beside me. She was singing to
herself, I remember, and then I opened my eyes.

45

Plato: For how long have I been gone?

Soul: It is hard to say.

Plato: Where did you find me?

Soul: Here. Among your papers.

Plato: It was a hard journey. It was as if I were enter-ing the cave and travelling beneath our earth. Could there have been such a place?

Soul: If you saw it, then it exists.

Plato: So it was not a vision? Or a dream?

Soul: What do you think?

Plato: I believe it to have been real.

Soul: And in turn I believe you. Of course, it may not be so easy to persuade the others.

Plato: Others?

Soul: But at least you have taken the first step. You have seen what was once unimaginable.

Plato: What is the saying? 'My eyes have been opened.' Now I must begin to wake my companions.

46

So you refuse to believe that I travelled to a dark cave in which the ancient inhabitants of London dwelled? Citizens, listen to me. Please listen. Perhaps I was mistaken. I had felt and believed that I was travelling beneath the earth, but that may have been my own lack of imagination. Perhaps they are all around us, but we cannot see one another. Now you are laughing again. You prove my point. It may be that we refuse to see them. Or they refuse to see us. I am not sure. Somehow we have all become separated. But I know this: our world and their world are intermingled.

47

Your own words condemn you. You confess to doubts about your journey and yet you expect us to believe your stories?

I have always taught stories. How our souls first came to light in the Age of Orpheus, when the divine human awoke from slumber and embraced us. How, in the malign Age of the Apostles, we learned to worship and suffer. I shall speak no more of Mouldwarp, but I have taught that the succeeding Age of Witspell witnessed a reawakening and restoration of human power. We look back at them with great attention. We have established an Academy for the sole purpose of studying

153

the beliefs of these past ages. But are we in a position to examine and to judge those who came before us? What if they are still examining us?

You are truly remarkable, Plato. You change your argument at every turn.

I am merely speculating. I assert nothing. It has always been my belief that speculation can do no harm.

It is not necessarily ours.

So, after all, I am to be condemned for challenging your beliefs? Then surely this age is no better than any that has come before.

Once more your head is filled with dreams and delusions.

Have you ever considered that our lives are a form of dream and that it is time to awake? What if we are being dreamed by the people of Mouldwarp? And what if we were dreaming them? What if the divine human had never woken and all the ages were part of the fabric of his sleep?

This is foolishness, Plato. Enough. We know that we exist. We know our history. We are not the figments of anyone's imagination.

Forgive me. I thought it was the city custom that I should be allowed to speak freely and openly in my defence. If I am permitted to reveal all that I have thought and imagined, after my journey, then perhaps the citizens will reject the charges of falsehood against me.

Yes. They signal their assent. It is allowed. Continue.

154

48

Sparkler: For so frail a figure, he has a powerful voice.

    Ornatus: No. Not powerful. Piercing. Somehow one always feels obliged to listen to him. He has always been full of ideas. I remember once, when we were children, he had a theory about the lambs of Lambeth. I cannot recall any of it now. I just remember his little face puckered up in sorrow, and his piping voice.

    Sparkler: Look. He is hitching up the sleeves of his robe.

    Ornatus: It has always been too large for him.

Sparkler: Did I tell you of my encounter with him, when I was about to be healed?

Ornatus: Of course. You have told everyone.

Sparkler: My apologies. Do you see his hands pointing upwards as he speaks? He is describing the old city again—

Ornatus: A phantom from his dreams.

Sparkler: Are you sure? He is describing its domes and high buildings and wide streets. There were once stars in a night sky. There was a sun, casting shadows upon the earth.

Ornatus: Next he will be saying that these shadows were souls.

Sparkler: You should not treat his story so lightly, Ornatus. What if all were true?

Ornatus: Why would it matter, true or not? One age is enough for me.

Sparkler: So you would prefer to remain in ignorance?

Ornatus: Ignorance is better than doubt.

Sparkler: Yet Plato has begun a process which will not end—

Ornatus: This is precisely why I condemn him. He has introduced uncertainty among us.

Sparkler: 'And if we doubt, the world goes out.' Who said that?

Ornatus: Can we please not discuss these matters? What is Plato doing now?

Sparkler: He is drawing some symbol or letter in the earth.

Ornatus: Absurd. Who can be expected to see it from here?

Sparkler: Do stop talking, Ornatus. Then we will be able to hear him. Look. Even the angels are interested. The tips of their wings have changed colour.

The people of Mouldwarp did not know why they believed in science. They knew only that it was absurd not to believe. And their science worked in their dimensions! They could move quickly from place to place, converse with one another over long distances, and see one another in different regions of the earth.

Ornatus: Three of the most foolish activities one can imagine.

Sparkler: Hush.

Science created a great reality for them. It manufactured planets, and stars, and medicines. Can we truly believe them to be primitive?

Ornatus: Oh yes. Certainly.

Sparkler: He speaks with great conviction.

Do you remember what one of the guardians told me during the first session? 'We do not wish to build our own monuments or memorials, since, unlike those who came before us, we wish to efface ourselves. All objects dissolve, so we choose not to make them.' Do you recall his words? Well, let me tell you this. We are astounded by our ancestors and their misconceptions, but we may seem equally foolish to our successors. In the distant villages of the hammer and the smith, as you know, dwell those who believe themselves to be already dead. They neither eat nor drink, but they survive their allotted span. May I prophesy? We will become like them, dying in life, if we refuse to countenance the presence of other realities around us.

Ornatus: This is madness. Can he truly believe what he says?

Sparkler: Do you see how some of the citizens are becoming restless?

Ornatus: Bewildered, too.

Sparkler: It is almost finished. The next session, according to custom, will also be the last.

Ornatus: I will be truly thankful.

49

Ours is a great and ancient city, with its own sacred rites. The citizens will assemble at the several gates, according to their parish, where the charges against you will once more be recited. Then they will sleep and, immediately on waking, they will know whether you are in a state of innocence or guilt. The spirit of the city will guide them. Of course you must then confer upon yourself whatever sentence you deem to be just. We have no part in that.

And should I decide to give orations as before?

That is your right. It will be after, not before, and that is *enough for us. It will not be the same city and you will not be the same person. Now, with your permission, may we draw these proceedings to a close?*

I am allowed a last petition, am I not?

If you wish it, then it is so. Proceed.

The Judgment
Upon Plato

50

Citizens who live beside the bishop's gate! You have heard how Plato defended himself and how he argued with the orators. What a vigorous performance that was! But how severely was he criticised for his excesses! In these great debates, however, you are the arbiters whose judgment abides. After taking part in the communal feast you will sleep and, when you awake, you will know the truth.

5 I

Sidonia: I'm afraid that I missed most of Plato's closing submission. Was it interesting?

Madrigal: Very fine indeed. It reminded me of our days at the Academy. There were many questions and interventions. Shall I try—

Sidonia: If you would.

Madrigal: Plato said:

Tell me, what is it that we presume to understand?
Ask any citizen and you will receive no true answer.

And yet we condemn past ages for their absurd beliefs! Ah. I am wrong again: we are certain of one thing. We know that for a while we are consigned to the wrong dimensions and that, at some point, they will pass away. There is a grief box in every parish where we can express our anxiety without being observed. I ask you if this is the way to live. I can no longer endure our patience, our endless worship, our expectation. Some of us grow old and fade. I have seen my own mother begin to depart, until she was scarcely visible even to me. Was this well done? Was this, in the words of the guardians, as it should be? I am not telling you that all is wrong, or all is well. I am simply asking you to question and, perhaps, to see the world in different ways. I have done so, upon my journey. I was stripped of all my certainties and felt physically afraid. But I survived, did I not? I want you to consider other possibilities. In that respect, at least, we may be more fortunate than those who came before us. I was once your orator. May I be permitted to impart one last lesson? I know that other ages, like that of Mouldwarp, refused to countenance or understand any reality but their own. That is why they perished. If we do not learn to doubt, then perhaps our own age will die. Now you are laughing at me again. Perhaps I have become a fool, to make you wise. What did you cry? I am out of harmony? I have always been so! Do you remember that in school we were taught that to be beautiful is to be virtuous? You see that I do not exactly fulfil the criterion of physical beauty. My body does not conform to the divine pattern of harmony. So I learned that I must follow my own path. You say that I have therefore departed from the proper way, but let me elucidate my own law of harmony. I would rather despise the whole world than be out of harmony with my own self. If others condemn me, then I will stand alone.

And that, Sidonia, is all I can remember.

52

You may sit or stand as you wish, Plato. This is the judgment of London. The citizens have decided that you are innocent of any attempt to corrupt the young. They have also concluded that you have not lied or prevaricated in your testimony. They believe that you suffered some fevered dream or hallucination while you lay among your papers. That is all. Your mask of oratory will be returned to you.

No. Wait. Is it not the custom that I should now pronounce sentence against myself?

But there is no sentence. You have not been charged with

any wrongdoing. The city has acquitted you. There is no more to say.

I understand that. If I may put it differently, there is no more for me to say. I have not been condemned as a liar or as an impostor, but I have been judged a dreamer or mistaken visionary who is not worthy of attention. All I have said or done is merely some fitful delusion. So now I pronounce sentence against myself. I cannot exist in a world which will ignore me or deride me—or, worse, pity me. I condemn myself to perpetual exile. I wish to be taken under escort beyond the walls of the city never to return.

This is madness.

But have I not been accused of madness already? What else could you expect from me but further folly? At least you will be rid of me.

We have no more authority in this matter, Plato. We are dissolved.

53

Plato: So you have been chosen to escort me beyond the walls.

Sidonia: Unhappily, yes. We are from the same parish, and I sat beside you in the Academy. What greater bond could exist? But, Plato, none of us has any wish to see you wander abroad.

Plato: I will wander and wonder. Perhaps I will find the old world again. Perhaps there is a cave or threshold in some distant place.

Sidonia: It was one of your suggestions at the trial.

Plato: Do you believe me, Sidonia? It is foolish of me, I suppose, but it would be some comfort to know that one of my childhood companions recognised the truth of my journey.

Sidonia: Are you sure that you believe it yourself?

Plato: It no longer matters what I believe.

Sidonia: You doubt yourself, and so you have spread doubt.

Plato: Our ancestors, Sidonia, were told that the first inhabitants of London were giants. There are stories of them carving great hills and valleys in which the city was planted. But what if this were prophecy, not history? What if we are the giants of which they had heard?

Sidonia: You are confusing me again.

Plato: Then it is better that I be gone and bother you no more.

Sidonia: Will you ever return?

Plato: Who can say?

Sidonia: You know, Plato, that I shall miss you.

Plato: Think of me as someone within a dream. Then I will never have left you.

54

Sparkler: Look. There he goes. Do you see how many children are following him down Lud Hill? You would think that he was leaving the city in triumph. Some of them are even giving him tokens of remembrance, to carry with him beyond the walls. The daughter of Ornatus is embracing him. But Plato is staring straight ahead, as if he were already considering his fate. Of course, that is it. Our world is already dead for him. He does not want to glance back in case his resolution falters.

Madrigal: Here comes the barge to take him down the Fleet. And Sidonia is sitting at the prow. What an unhappy expedition for her! Listen to the children singing by the banks of the river, as he steps on board the vessel. Do you see how its sails gleam against the waters? Now Plato is raising his hands in farewell. But, Sparkler, I have just noticed something. Why have the angels stayed away?

55

So Plato left the city and was never seen again. There are many who say that he travelled to other cities, where he continued his orations. Some are convinced that there was indeed a cave beneath the earth and that Plato returned there unknown and unseen by the people of Mouldwarp. Sidonia and Ornatus believe that he simply entered another dream.